"Don't you ha need to tell me?

"I don't know what you are talking about."

"Don't you?" He stared into Alex's eyes. "Where is the child?" he asked firmly.

Even though she'd known what he was there for all along, that sent a shock through her system.

"What child?" she said breathlessly, fighting for equilibrium.

He pulled her close.

"The baby you had five months ago in Paris. Where are you keeping him?

She closed her eyes, feeling faint. Her head was reeling. He knew more than she'd thought. There wasn't much she could do but bluster her way through this.

Opening her eyes, she glared at him. His blue eyes were searching her face, as though he would find answers in her gaze.

"Alex, we were together at exactly the right time to make this my business."

She shook her head firmly. "You don't know that."

He captured her chin in his hand, tilting her face to receive him. "I do know," he said softly, then lowered his lips to hers.

She tried to find the wherewithal to resist, but it was no use. His mouth felt so warm, so good, and she opened to his kiss as though she'd been starving for him.

Dear Reader

This is an exciting year for romance writers and fans. Mills & Boon is celebrating a very special birthday—one hundred years of publishing great fiction. If you go to the websites for Mills & Boon and Harlequin, you'll find out more about the festivities, as well as lots of fun facts about romance through the years.

In the meantime, those of you who have been following the story of the restored Montenevada monarchy will be happy to know Crown Prince Dane has found his missing baby. Luckily, the mother of this royal baby is the woman Dane loves. Sometimes life *does* work out the way it should.

But wait! Not so fast! Things can't be that easy. Alexandra may be the woman he's loved for years, but she's also an Acredonna, and the daughter of the man who originally wrested the little European country of Carnethia away from Dane's people. The bad blood between these families is poisoned with bitterness, old and new. Even if the two lovers can get beyond personal animosities, will the people ever accept a match between them? Will Crown Prince Dane have to give up the country he was meant to rule in order to marry Alexandra? Or will he do his duty and live without love?

Hope you enjoy finding out the answer. Happy reading!

Raye Morgan

FOUND:
HIS ROYAL BABY

BY
RAYE MORGAN

MILLS & BOON®

Pure reading pleasure™

First published in Great Britain 2008
Harlequin Mills & Boon Limited,
Eton House, 18-24 Paradise Road, Richmond, Surrey TW9 1SR

© Helen Conrad 2008

ISBN: 978 0 263 86545 5

Set in Times Roman 13 on 15½ pt
02-1008-43790

Printed and bound in Spain
by Litografia Rosés, S.A., Barcelona

THE ROYALS OF MONTENEVADA

Three gorgeous princes…
and how they meet their brides-to-be!

The whole kingdom is in an uproar. As the princes
fulfil their duties, a rumour starts that one special
woman is carrying a royal heir. A massive search
reveals three single mothers…who might be perfect
for the three Montenevada sons. Could love be
part of the royal baby bargain?

Find out in August–October 2008, with this
exciting new mini-series by Raye Morgan:

THE PRINCE'S SECRET BRIDE: Meet Nico, who
never expects to encounter a pregnant woman with
amnesia…much less marry her!

ABBY AND THE PLAYBOY PRINCE: Mychale
discovers a tempting woman living in his house, then
finds out she's hiding a secret baby…

FOUND: HIS ROYAL BABY: Dane never forgot
her, then learned they had a child together. Can they
finally become the family he's always wanted?

To Repaircat Jack, for all the Fix-its!

CHAPTER ONE

CROWN Prince Dane of the Royal House of Montenevada, newly reinstalled monarchy of the sovereign nation of Carnethia, walked reluctantly into the trendy dance club. Chic's was located in a neighboring country to his own, in the nightlife district of the city of Darnam. The pulsing music seemed to slam against his brain like a bad headache. The swirling colors and flashing lights brought back painful memories of nights on the battlefield—nights not so far removed but best left unremembered.

He stood at the entry, waiting for his eyes to adjust to the light, scanning the crowd. He was alone. He'd ditched his security detail at his hotel and headed out on his own without company. There was nothing about him to signal royalty, but people turned and looked at him, anyway. Standing at the top of the stairs, his thick dark hair slightly tousled, his legs apart, his hands lightly clenched, his tough, muscular body balanced, he would have looked like a fighter if his face hadn't been so flawlessly handsome. Few in this crowd seemed to recognize who he was, but they knew he was someone—someone of consequence. And they stared at him, wondering.

He began to walk through the crowd, his startling silver-blue eyes searching. Men stepped back out of his way, suddenly wary, as though they sensed danger. Women followed him with their gazes, unconsciously flirting with their eyes, their lips, the way they thrust out their breasts as he passed. But he didn't make contact. He was looking for someone, like a hunter stalking prey.

A champagne cork popped, the explosion sending golden bubbles through the air. Someone at the far end of the room was calling out a toast, and confetti began to fall from the ceiling. He turned slowly, staring at the boisterous group. Two people stepped back, parting the crowd, and there she was in the center of everything.

He froze, still as a statue. She was just as he'd remembered her: thick, mahogany-red hair swirled riotously around her beautiful face in deep, extravagant curls; eyes as green as precious emeralds glittered beneath long dark lashes, all set against skin as white and pure as alabaster. Her dress was cut low enough to reveal a lot of smooth, luscious skin. Made of something slinky, it was shaped trim and tight in the bodice and around her full, lavish hips, only to whirl out around her knees, giving a generous view of her perfect, athletically muscular legs. She was still the most gorgeous creature he'd ever seen.

But seeing her again drove a knife into his heart. Real, physical pain sliced through his body. For just a moment, this man who had stood up to armies and assassins without a qualm was flooded with the instinct to turn and run. Facing her like this was hard. If it hadn't been for his suspicions about her, he would have stayed away. But he was pretty sure she had something that belonged to him. This was a stand he had to take.

He watched as she laughed up at the so-phisticated-looking man with silver hair at his temples who was standing next to her. The man smiled down at her as though he had a claim. Dane raised an eyebrow. Another dragon to slay?

No matter. He'd come on a mission and he wasn't going to be deterred. But as the man reached out and put his hand on the woman's naked upper arm, a feeling like cold anger twisted inside Dane. His heart, which had been thudding harder than usual, but at a steady pace, began to bang against his chest wall. Adrenaline. He always felt like this before a fight.

The people around her had fallen silent, watching his approach, and finally she turned and saw him. Her gaze met his and caught, held by the intensity in his eyes. It was one of those crystal moments that would be seared into his soul for a lifetime. For just a few seconds, time stood still. Everything else faded away—all the people, the music, the noise, even breathing itself. There was only the two of them and the deep, tangled connection that sizzled between them.

And then her green eyes widened and her mouth opened as though she might almost cry out. And that was when he saw the fear.

She covered it up quickly. Her chin rose and her eyes flashed defiant fire. But he'd seen the truth. She didn't fear much, but she was afraid of him. And if she feared him, there could only be one reason. It meant his guess was right.

It was an educated guess. He'd heard rumors and he'd put two and two together. He'd been shown pictures, but pictures could be faked.

Still, he had to admit, hope had come into play. But he didn't think he'd let it carry him away. He knew a reliance on hope brought only heartbreak. He'd spent a lifetime learning to control his emotions. Hell, some might even say he'd learned to snuff out any communication with his heart. It had a basic function, to keep pumping vitality into his body. As for the rest, he'd learned to live without it. Life was simpler that way.

She tossed back thick, silky hair that glowed with deep-red highlights, scattering confetti that had caught in it as she did so. Squaring her shoulders, she faced him boldly.

"So, what do we have here?" she said in a sort of mock greeting. "The pretender to the Carnethian throne, isn't it?"

He gazed back steadily. "I'm not the pretender, Alexandra. You Acredonnas were the pretenders." He put his hand over his heart as he added coolly, "I'm the real thing."

All the fire and pain of the war stood between them, the war during which his family, the Montenevadas, took back the country her family, the Acredonnas, had wrested from them fifty years before.

"I want to talk to you," he told her.

The smile that twisted her carmine lips held no hint of warmth. "Interesting. But this is a dance club. I want to dance."

He shrugged, his eyes hooded. "I'm at your service."

That seemed to surprise her. A look of wariness flashed in her green eyes.

"Not with you," she said, a bit too quickly.

He raised an eyebrow. "Why not? What are you afraid of?"

"Not you," she said again, eyes narrowing. "Never you."

But there was a thread of quivering emotion in her voice that gave lie to her declaration. Something in him responded to it, softening. His impulse was to reach for her, and his hand went out to do just that.

Too late. The tall man with the silver sideburns had come to her side, and she stared at Dane's hand as if it were a snake. Quickly she took the tall man's arm, leaning into him as though for protection.

"I'm all booked up, you see," she told Dane flippantly. "Maybe some other time."

He shrugged, dropping his hand to his side. "I'll wait," he said, not allowing her to see evidence of the ache that tore through him at her rejection.

The tall man flashed Dane a look of pure triumph, but he ignored it. The man was nothing. A mere annoyance. Alexandra was in his sights and she was all he was focused on. He leaned against a post, arms folded, and watched them go out onto the tiny, crowded dance floor.

They were good. It was obvious they'd

danced together before. He watched her turn and shimmer to the music, and he cursed the way it made him feel. She moved like an angel with just enough fire to be an arousing delight, but not so much as to lose that simple, decent elegance that he'd always seen in her. She moved like a lady—a provocative lady, but a lady, nonetheless.

His mouth went dry as he watched her. He wanted her. He always wanted her. This was his fatal flaw, the chink in his armor, the weak place in his soul. If he wasn't careful, it could destroy him.

Every muscle in his body hardened. Somehow this woman appealed to him in ways no other female had ever come close to. And here she was, the enemy. Their families had fought against each other for decades. She hated him. She'd made that very plain every time they'd met. He knew there could never be anything but fierce animosity between them.

Still, for some reason, people were always telling him what she was up to, where she was, who she was seeing. No matter how often he ordered them into silence, somehow they managed to convey every rumor that poisoned the air. And one rumor in particular had chilled his blood. That was the one he had to check out. Once he'd heard of it, he knew he couldn't stay away.

Alex and her brothers had been difficult to find since they'd escaped from Carnethia at the end of war. He'd heard only that morning that she might be coming to Chic's tonight, in this small, neighboring neutral country. Interestingly, it had been his sister, Carla, who had told him, in casual conversation over toast, and not the intelligence people he'd specifically tasked for the last few weeks with the job of finding her—ever since he'd heard the whispers about her and what she'd been doing for the last year or so.

She came back to the table with cheeks stained red and a new sparkle in her green eyes.

"Are you still here?" she asked as she passed him.

"I'm still here. We need to talk."

She glanced back at him over her shoulder. "I don't think—"

His hand flashed out and took her upper arm in his grip, fingers curling tightly into her soft flesh. Two men in her party reacted quickly, stepping forward and looking to her for a sign.

"I *do* think," Dane said crisply, ignoring her protectors. "Either you dance with me, or I'm taking you out into the street. One way or another, we're going to talk."

She glared at him. "You're not royalty here, Dane. Everyone doesn't tremble at your every desire."

His lip curled. "Too bad. You look so appealing when you tremble."

Her breath caught in her throat and she blinked rapidly, trying hard to keep her cool. What he'd said had connotations far beyond this room, and the reminder set her back on her heels. He knew just how to get to her, to reach in and find the weak spot.

And he was bound and determined to be a jerk tonight, wasn't he? She was caught in a trap. She had bodyguards with her, but she couldn't let them make a scene. Things were too dicey for her family in this city as it was.

Too late she had a pang of regret. She shouldn't have come tonight. She'd only chanced it because she was so sick of hiding. But she should have known this might happen.

Oh, why didn't she just admit it? She'd hoped against all reason that she would see him. Or see someone who knew him. Or at least hear something about him. Even though she knew any kind of contact was the most dangerous thing for her.

But it had been so long and she hungered for him in ways she couldn't reveal. Every scrap of information she could find fed her addiction to the man. She had pictures, mostly of official royal functions where he'd appeared recently. And she had his T-shirt, the one he'd been wearing when she'd found him in the wreck of his car and dragged him to safety. It was still stained with his blood, because to wash it would be to wash away the scent of him, the feel of him, the knowledge that it had once been against his body.

But all this had to be in secret, because she could never have the man himself. And to let him near her like this was stupidly reckless.

Still, she was surrounded by friends. He couldn't do anything to her here. So why did she feel so vulnerable? Why did fear flutter inside her like a butterfly seeking freedom?

She had to do something. Dane was going to make sure she was humiliated if he kept this up. The only way to avoid it was going to be to dance with the man. Very well, then. She took a deep breath and raised her chin. She might as well get it over with.

"You win, oh mighty one," she said mockingly. "Let's dance."

Second thoughts came fast and furious, and she stiffened as he took her in his arms as though they were heading out to perform a Viennese waltz. She hadn't expected that.

"Wait," she said, resisting. "What are you doing?"

"You don't think I'm going to do the Shim Sham or whatever crazy dance is popular, do you?" he said blithely, not giving an inch. "I'm not one of your pretty boys, Alexandra. And I won't make a spectacle of myself before the whole world."

She lifted her chin, green eyes glittering. "You didn't like my dancing style?"

He smiled down at her coldly. "Your dancing was exotic, erotic and totally shameless."

He pulled her just a bit closer. The music started and he began to lead her onto the dance floor, turning her slowly to every other beat. Somehow, it worked, and though they were in a slow embrace, they seemed to be in tune to the music, regardless.

"I told you I wanted to talk. We can't do that jumping up and down on each other's toes."

Her pulse raced. It was so strange to be with him like this. For months she'd longed to see him at the same time she dreaded it. Now that he was here, she knew nothing good could come of it. He was a danger to her, a danger to her family. She had to be so careful what she said, so careful what she let him know. He was still the enemy, no matter what ties still lingered between them.

And here she was, so close to him she could feel his breath in her hair. Her gaze drifted to the open neck of his white shirt. She remembered what that chest looked like without a shirt, she remembered…

"Oh!" She pulled back, closing her eyes against the vision. "I thought you wanted to talk," she said quickly. "Go ahead. Say something."

"I was trying to recall if we'd ever danced together before," he said softly.

"Never," she snapped. "And this will be the only time, so make the most of it."

"You're wrong," he said, his voice a low rumble in his chest. "Don't you remember that hotel cocktail lounge in Tokyo?"

She looked up and met his steady gaze, even though she knew it was a big mistake. Tokyo was over six years ago. They'd been so young, and both dispatched by their families as representatives to the International Conference on Economic Growth.

They'd started out antagonists when he'd made an official challenge to her right to sit for Carnethia. He'd called her family's rule illegitimate, he'd called her a usurper. She'd reacted angrily, calling him a sore loser, a remnant of a decadent past. They'd come face-to-face, staring each other down.

They'd carried their argument into the dining room during the official banquet, and then into the meeting rooms, and finally into the cocktail lounge. And somehow they had ended up dancing. And dancing. The night went on and on. The antagonism had melted away, but not the passion. Once they'd come together like that, they couldn't seem to keep away from each other. They spent most of the next two days in each other's arms.

By the time they had boarded separate planes Monday morning, she could have sworn they were in love. That it was forever. That nothing could keep them apart. She could hardly wait to get home to begin making plans. She knew it wouldn't be easy to convince her family that love was more important than old grudges, but she was sure she would find a way.

But she'd been wrong. There was no way. She'd been dreaming of bridal veils and satin wedding gowns, and her country had been taking up arms. While they'd been gone, romancing in Tokyo, the unrest in Carnethia had taken a serious turn for the worse. Fighting had begun along the border. The world of Acredonna power that she'd grown up being so sure of was quickly crumbling, though she didn't know it yet.

She was swept up in the fight almost immediately, and Dane was the enemy, one of the leaders of the very people who were trying to ruin her family. She didn't see him again until the last month of the war.

The war was over now, but the bitterness lingered on.

"Tokyo?" she lied, shrugging. "I don't remember Tokyo. Ancient history."

He winced. Beyond all reason, that was another painful twist to his heart.

"I've been searching for you for weeks," he said gruffly. "You and your family have kept a low profile since the war ended."

"That's what happens to the vanquished, isn't it?" She looked up into his eyes. "The losers have to hide."

Her eyes had always had the power to hypnotize him. Once he looked into them, he had a hard time looking away. But there was something different tonight. The usual open honesty she gave him was missing. Something furtive hid in the recesses of those beautiful irises. He searched hard, trying to analyze what she was avoiding. But he was pretty sure he knew what it was.

"And your father?" he asked with real curiosity. There were so many rumors floating around and so few solid facts.

"My father?" A flash of anger covered her wariness. "What do you care about my father? You hate him."

"He's been a big influence on my life, whatever the reason. I'm curious. I've heard different things and I'd like to know what the real story is."

She pressed her lips together, then decided to tell him the truth. "My father is sick and barely hanging on."

He drew in a sharp breath. "I'm sorry," he murmured.

She grunted skeptically, shrugging away his simple sympathy. "And he is very, very bitter."

He shrugged. He'd assumed that. "Of course."

She took a deep breath, glanced into his eyes and then away. "Mostly toward his own children," she admitted, "who were not able to hang on to the prize he won for the family fifty years ago."

He nodded. He took that as a matter of course as well. His father would have been the same, had he lived and gone through what her father had suffered.

"And yet, you're here," he noted dryly.

She nodded, biting her lip. "It's my birthday."

Her birthday. He almost caught his breath at that news. Why it should affect him with a wave of emotion he wasn't sure, but it did.

"I didn't bring you a present," he said softly.

She looked up at him, her lower lip quivering, but her eyes still full of spirit. "And here I thought you considered yourself a gift to the human race," she said flippantly.

"Cute."

He looked at her mouth. The urge to kiss her surged in his chest. The music stopped and they stood swaying, still pressed together. He stared at the way her lip was trembling, so full and delicious and tempting.

And below, the full thrust of her breasts, the deep, shadowed cleavage between them. He could feel the warmth rising from it, taste the heat he would find in her mouth. Every fiber of his being wanted her. No other woman would ever affect him the way she did.

And no woman was more impossible for him to have.

His head went back as he realized the

murmurs had begun. Someone had recognized him, and the whispers were spreading
through the hall. This sort of thing was
familiar to him—happened all the time. He
wouldn't be able to stay much longer.

The flash from a paparazzi camera blinded
him for a moment, anchoring him back to
earth. Exactly what he hated most, the
tabloid culture and their vultures. He swore
softly, then drew back, still holding her hand.

"Obviously, this was a bad idea. We can't
talk here." He looked at her questioningly.
"Unless you want to just go ahead and tell me
the truth."

"Truth? Why, Your Highness, you know I
never lie."

For some contrary reason, that made him
smile.

"Good. Then I'm sure you'll be ready to
tell me everything tomorrow when we can
get some privacy." He gave her a quick chuck
under the chin. "I'll see you then," he told
her. "Where are you staying?"

She stared at him, seemingly startled out
of all ability to speak.

"Never mind. I'll find out. Nine-thirty at

your hotel. We'll talk then. You order in coffee, I'll bring the brioche."

Turning on his heel, he walked past the photographer who was still snapping pictures. His hand shot out and grabbed the camera before the man knew what was happening.

"Hey!" the paparazzo yelled out.

Dane flipped him a business card. "Call this number in the morning," he said. "You'll get your camera back. In the meantime, I'll babysit it for you."

"Hey," the man yelled again, following but not quite daring to do anything about it. "You can't do that!"

But he'd already done it, and he was out the door and into his waiting Aston Martin before anyone could stop him.

CHAPTER TWO

ALEXANDRA Acredonna, only daughter of Luther Acredonna, recently deposed leader of the Nationalists, whose rule of Carnethia was ended by Crown Prince Dane, his father and his brothers, was in despair.

It had been a huge mistake to come out in public. She shouldn't have risked it. It had been so long, and she'd been so hungry for some sort of social contact, that when some dear friends had invited her to a birthday celebration at Chic's, she'd been too tempted to turn the offer down. She'd gone, swearing she would only be at the club for an hour, in and out, gone before there would be time for anyone to notice her and send out the word.

But it hadn't worked out that way. Dane had obviously been tipped off. Which meant there might be someone in her entourage who was giving information to the Montenevadas. A chilling thought. If they had leaked once, they would leak again.

She stared into the dressing room mirror, trying to concentrate on solutions. She had to be supersecret and supercareful from now on. She was going to have to become more disciplined. Ridding herself of all the people around her was the first step. Only one or two of her closest advisors should know where she was at any given time.

She was staying at the Lion's Mane Hotel here in Darnam. It was a huge place and she'd registered under an assumed name and taken one of the cheaper suites for her party, so she'd thought she would be lost in the shuffle.

No such luck. Now she was back in the hotel room, looking forward to a long, sleepless night and wondering who among her people might be a traitor.

But most of all, she was thinking about Dane.

She'd been shocked to see him standing there in the club. He'd looked good—healthier than when she'd seen him last. Her heart had seemed to jump in her chest when she saw him. Every cell, every nerve, came more alive than ever. She saw things, felt things, she didn't see or feel when he wasn't near. She knew she would never be free of the emotions he conjured up in her just by being within reach.

The way he'd looked at her! The way his blue eyes had penetrated her self-confidence and stripped her to the bone. For a moment she'd been afraid she had no defense against him. But she'd regained her balance quickly enough and pushed through that to find her inner strength.

Still, she knew now that he was on to her. He'd heard things. He probably wasn't sure of the facts yet. If he'd been sure, he would have done more than dance around the subject. He would have grabbed her, thrown her over his shoulder and carried her out of that place if he'd known for certain that she'd had his child. And next time, that was probably what he would do.

Her cell phone rang and she picked it up, expecting to see one of her brothers' numbers on the screen. But no. The number wasn't one she recognized. Again her heart began to thump in her chest. It had to be Dane.

She wouldn't answer. She'd just let it ring. Biting her lip, she tried to stand firm on that. One more ring and she crumbled.

"Hello?" she said breathlessly.

For a beat or two there was silence.

"Did I wake you?" he said at last, and she let out a breath she hadn't realized she'd been holding.

"Of course not," she managed to say airily. "But you are interrupting," she added, lying through her teeth and unapologetic about it. "I'm having a nightcap with a…friend," she added, making sure to imply the friend was male.

He chuckled. "No, you're not."

She hadn't thought he could get more infuriating, but she'd been wrong.

"Prove it," she demanded. "How could you possibly know what I'm doing in my own hotel room?"

"Prove that you're not two-timing me with someone else?" he said mockingly. "Isn't that *your* role?"

That statement was too outrageous to challenge. He might as well have accused her of having an affair with a Martian. She wasn't even going to dignify it with a comment. At least, she knew she shouldn't. But in the end, she was just too irritated to let it pass.

"How could I be two-timing a man I haven't seen for six years until tonight?" she demanded reasonably.

"Are you going to ignore that week during the last month of the war?"

She drew her breath in sharply, wondering how much he remembered, how much he was just fishing in the dark. "I don't know what you're talking about."

"I think you do, Alex. I'm sure you remember more about our last encounter than I do. I was unconscious most of the time, after all." His voice hardened. "But bits and pieces of that scene are beginning to clear up for me. And what I'm looking at presents quite an interesting picture."

She closed her eyes, wishing she knew how to convince him to drop his probing. Wasn't there something she could say, something she could imply? "Your imagination is working overtime."

"You think so? Well, that's exactly what we need to talk about. See you in the morning."

"Wait," she said, her fingers clenching the cell phone tightly. "How did you get my number?"

"I'm the head of state of a country with an intelligence service, Alex. You should remember that. Your family used to be in charge here, and I know you had one. Our people are a little rusty, but they're getting the hang of these things."

"Of course," she said softly.

"See you in the morning," he said again.

She closed her phone without answering.

She shivered, her heart in her throat. It was time she faced facts. She was at such a disadvantage. He had all the power now, and she had none. If he knew the truth, if he was sure, he would find ways to take her baby from her. She had to do something to protect him, to protect herself.

She would take measures. She would become even more elusive. She would dye her hair and wear a veil and…and…

She groaned. No matter. He would find her. And he would find the truth. It was only a matter of time. What could she do?

Run. That was the only thing she could think of. Run and hide and keep running.

For how long?

She closed her eyes.

For as long as it took.

"Excuse me, miss."

She looked up. Grace, the new nanny, was in the doorway looking hesitant. Or was she looking guilty? Was she the one who'd snitched? Alex winced. Was she going to have to go through the rest of her life not trusting anyone?

"What is it, Grace?" she asked.

"I know it's late, but the baby's fussing a bit. I thought maybe…"

She nodded, feeling her milk come in. The anticipation of holding her child made her smile despite everything. "Of course. I'll be right there."

Baby Robbie was the one shining bit of happiness in her life. Just looking at his precious little face gave her hope.

But he was hers and hers alone. She would never let Dane take him away from her. Never.

She woke from a dream, gasping. Was the man even going to haunt her sleep? She shuddered, trying to erase the erotic turn her subconscious fantasies had taken. True to her fears, she'd only slept a few hours.

Closing her eyes, she quickly went over all the possibilities. She could foresee what his next move would be. A normal man might have begun by charming her and trying to convince her that he deserved to know the truth, and that once he knew the truth, he would act reasonably and fairly and wouldn't do anything rash.

But Dane couldn't promise all those things, because Dane wasn't reasonable and fair. He wasn't going to ask her to sign papers or make agreements. He was going to try to force her to tell him what he wanted to know, and if she didn't comply right away, he would do something to convince her she had no choice. And then he would find a way to take her baby.

Panic shot through her and she held herself tightly, rocking back and forth. What was she going to do? How was she going to protect herself from that?

It didn't matter how many obstacles she put up or how many security guards she had around her, Dane would find a way to break through all that. There was only one answer. She had to make a move before he did.

What was she still doing here? She knew she had to leave before Dane got here in the morning. She might as well get the show on the road. There was nothing important keeping them here.

The only problem was she didn't want to take many of them with her. Grace, the nanny, of course. And Henri and Kavon, her personal guards. The rest could go back to Paris.

Yes, she told herself as she rose and began to dress. She had to leave. She had to get out before Dane arrived. Just before going to bed, she'd had word that her brothers, Marque and Ivan, were on their way to Darnam as well, and she didn't want to risk seeing them before she went into hiding. She knew they were probably coming to try to enlist her in their latest wild scheme to get back at Dane and his family. One of these days they just might gather enough of a force together to do the Montenevadas real harm, but she didn't want to be involved. It was time to declare the war over.

Should she pack? There was no time. Now that she'd thought over all the ramifications, she wanted to hurry, to run, to dash out the door, her baby in her arms, straight to a hiding place.

She called Henri on her phone. He was her ever-alert, ever-faithful one and she knew the older man would be awake in the next room.

"I'm up," he said. "I'm ready to go. I was hoping you would see the wisdom in it."

Quickly, she went over plans with him and he agreed to take care that the others left for Paris right away.

"One thing," he said. "I've heard your brothers are heading here to join you. Should I let them know…?"

"No," she said quickly. "I don't want them to know what we're doing. I'll call them later, once we get there."

"The usual place?" he asked carefully.

"Of course."

It was settled. She felt energized, now that she saw a clear path in front of her. She woke the nanny and went in to change Robbie's diapers and prepare him for the trip. As always, she found herself forgetting her worries and smiling as she tended to him. He gurgled and cooed. What a love he was.

"Hurry, Grace," she urged. "We've got to get on the road."

Her brothers. What if they did come here? She wanted to avoid them almost as much as she'd wanted to avoid Dane, whom they hated with a passion. They might even kill him if they found him here. At the very least, they would harm him, and despite everything, she couldn't stand the thought of it. Should she warn him somehow? Leave a note? Make a call?

Closing her eyes, she laughed softly. See how crazy she was getting? Even as she was running from the man, she was thinking of his welfare.

"Are you ready?" she called in to Grace.

"Just a moment more," the girl called back. "I'll be there."

Alex sighed, rocking her baby in her arms. Soon they would be safe. Very soon.

The sun hadn't made an appearance yet as Dane knocked, then waited patiently for the young man to come and open the outer door to the Lion's Mane service entrance for him. The employee handed him a small ring of keys and he handed back a folded bill. Nodding, he took the back stairs and climbed quickly to the fifth floor, then used the keys to unlock the service door and let himself onto the floor.

He paused, listening at the double doors. She would have a full party of servants and escorts in her entourage, but they wouldn't all be staying here on this floor with her. He figured two or three guards at the most. He was hoping to avoid them, but if the muffled sounds he heard were any indication, they were already up and probably getting ready to head out of town. Good thing he'd come early.

Another twist of a key and he was inside the suite of rooms being used by the Acredonna party, standing in the wide entryway that had three rooms leading from it. His heart was pounding but he wasn't sure if that was because of the danger involved or the prospect of seeing her again. He chose one of the rooms on instinct, walking softly to the doorway. And there she was.

She didn't see him at first. She was dressed in jeans and a bright, tucked-in shirt that was full in the sleeves. Her hair was loose in a glorious riot of red curls. She was bending over a pile of CDs, reading labels and pulling two out of the stack.

"It's getting late," she said without turning as she sensed the presence of another person in the room. "Did you bring the car around?"

"No," he responded softly. "And I forgot to bring the brioche as well."

Dropping the CDs, she whirled, hand to her mouth as though to stop a scream. "Oh!" she gasped, her eyes huge.

He smiled, soaking in the sight of her. "You're even beautiful at four in the morning," he noted. "But then, I knew that."

The tension between them was electric.

"What are you doing here?"

He shrugged casually, but his eyes were alert, following every nuance of her reactions.

"Keeping track of you is like trying to catch a rainbow in your hand. I thought I'd better get here early." His smile faded and he regarded her narrowly. "It looks like that was a wise decision on my part."

She glanced back at the doorway nervously. "I have guards with me, you know."

He looked at the doorway, too, sure that was where any attacker would be coming from and planning accordingly. It was automatic, second nature. The only thing that might get in the way of his natural protective radar was this woman who seemed to be able to cloud his senses as though she wore a magic perfume.

"Of course," he said to her. "Are you going to order them to throw me out?"

She hesitated and he could see that she would love to do just that, if she thought she could get away with it.

"Not if you behave," she said at last.

He made a short bow. "You have my word. I promise not to ravish you right here on the Persian carpet. Is that enough?"

"Be serious." She took a deep breath, steadying herself. "I'm afraid we aren't going to have time to have that talk," she said, making an attempt to sound light-hearted and failing utterly. "We've decided we must leave right away. So…"

One quick step closed the gap between them. He moved before she had time to react and took her hand in his, looking down into her startled eyes.

"Alexandra, you're not going anywhere until we have our talk. We've got things we need to clarify between us. You know that."

She tried to pull her hand away but he wasn't going to let it go.

"Don't you have something you need to tell me?" he asked.

"I don't know what you're talking about."

"Don't you?" He stared into her eyes. "Where is the child?" he asked firmly.

Even though she'd known what he was here for all along, that sent a shock through her system.

"What child?" she said breathlessly, fighting for equilibrium.

He pulled her closer, staring intently into her eyes.

"The baby you had five months ago in Paris. Where are you keeping him?"

She lifted her chin defiantly.

"That's just nonsense." She felt stronger as she fought back. "Who told you I had a baby?"

He looked pained. "Alex, please. People tell me all kinds of things. I have to sift through a lot of lies to get to the few kernels of truth. I've had a lot of experience at this."

"Then what makes you think you've got hold of some good information for a change?" she demanded, trying to buy time.

"More than one trusted source." He shrugged. He'd only recently gathered enough evidence to know he was on firm ground. "I've seen proof. You had a baby just about five months ago at the Sisters of Mercy private clinic on Gereaux Street, the little building behind the art gallery. I've seen pictures."

She closed her eyes, feeling faint. Her head was reeling. He had more than she'd thought. There wasn't much she could do but bluster her way through this.

Opening her eyes again, she glared at him.

"Even if I did have a baby, what business is it of yours?"

His blue eyes were searching her face as though he would find answers in her gaze.

"Alex, we were together at exactly the right time to make it my business."

She shook her head firmly. "You don't know that. You can't remember what happened to you during your recovery. You've said so again and again. It's even been in the papers."

He hesitated. "It's true. I have very little memory of that period of my life. I was unconscious most of the time."

"There, you see? Then what makes you think...?"

"Certain memories are coming back." He touched her cheek with the palm of his hand, and his gaze softened as it traced her hairline. "Memories of skin like silk and hair like fire," he murmured.

She stiffened, determined not to let him get to her. "Maybe you were dreaming."

"No." He shook his head. "No, Alex." His fingers touched her small, shell-like ear, then curled softly around it. "I remember how you taste. I remember you slipping into my bed, soft and willing and..."

"No!" She tried to pull away, but his hand held hers like a vise.

"You tasted like fine wine."

She rolled her eyes. "Oh, please. That's crazy. Women all taste alike."

His smile was slight but deadly. She shivered, wishing she had the strength to look away.

"No, they don't," he said. "No one else tastes like you do."

Her heart was thudding in her throat, beating so hard she could hardly breathe. "How would you know that? It's…it's been years, and then you were wounded and…"

He captured her chin in his hand, tilting her face to receive him. "I'll show you," he said softly, then lowered his lips to hers.

She tried to gather the wherewithal to resist, but it was no use. His mouth felt so warm, so good, and she opened to his kiss as though she'd been starving for him.

But it only lasted for a moment. He drew back and looked at her, shaking his head. "Alex," he began.

But she never heard what he was about to say. Her attention was caught by something behind him on the other side of the room. Henri was there, his long, thin body bent over, a tranquilizer gun raised and trained on his target. He was going to shoot a dart into Dane.

Of course. It was the only way they could possibly get out of here without Dane and his security people following them. Good for Henri. Quick thinking. It made sense. And yet the feelings that filled her were over-whelming. She couldn't do this. She had so much hidden affection for this man, despite everything. She couldn't let him be hurt in any way.

"No!" she cried out to Henri. "Wait!"

Dane looked at her, startled, and by the time he realized there was someone else in the room, it was too late. The dart had been shot from the tranquilizer gun. He looked at her in disbelief, reached back to try to pull out the dart, swore and crumpled to the floor.

"Did you hurt him?" she cried, though she knew the question was moot. Dropping to the floor, she swept his hair back off his forehead and searched his unconscious face for signs. "Didn't you hear me say to wait?"

Henri shrugged. Leaning down, he pulled out the dart and noted it was empty. The fluid would do its work.

"I couldn't risk it. He had to be rendered harmless." He reached for her hand. "Come on. Let's get out of here."

"No." She rose, looking down at the prince. Emotion choked her throat. "We can't leave him like this."

Henri looked at her, incredulous. "What are you talking about? We have to go. He might have others outside. And in any case, your brothers will be here soon. You don't want to have to talk to them about this, do you?"

"No." She put a hand to her head, trying to sort things out. "We must go. But…"

"Come along, then. Grace is already in the car with the baby. I'll tell the manager to hold our bags and things in storage until we send for them."

She nodded, still looking down at where Dane lay like a wounded stag.

"We have to take him with us," she said softly, a feeling of wonderment growing inside her. How could she even think of such a thing? And yet, there wasn't any choice.

"If we leave him here…" A few horrendous consequences flashed through her mind. She looked up at Henri. "Don't you see?"

He looked pained, his thin face haggard. "Your brothers…"

"Yes." She threw a hand out, half in a sense of command, half beseeching him to understand. "Who knows what they would do to him?"

"But, miss, we can't," he said, his usually stoic expression twisted into a special sort of agony. "What are we going to do with him? What will he do when he comes to? Don't you see how dangerous that would be?"

She stared into his worried eyes. "But don't you see how impossible it is to leave him?" she said simply.

He stared back and what he saw in her eyes seemed to explain it all to him. Slowly he nodded, and a look of resignation began to relax his face.

"All right, then," he said, resolved and back to being the normal unflappable paragon of efficiency. "I'll take care of it. You go."

"No." She shook her head, tears trembling in her eyes. It wasn't that she didn't trust him. It was just that she couldn't bear to risk anything happening to Dane. She had to be involved. All the way.

"No, I'll help carry him. I'd rather."

He nodded curtly. "Let's do it, then."

CHAPTER THREE

ALEXANDRA stared at her reflection in the mirror and wondered who that was looking back. She looked haunted, scared, hopeless. And she needed to appear calm and cool and collected. Could she be all those things at once?

Hardly.

Things were rapidly careening out of control. She'd done the unthinkable—brought the crown prince of Carnethia to her only hideout, the only place where she was sure she could be safe. She'd brought the man she was hiding from right into the heart of her refuge. What was she thinking?

But no matter how crazy it seemed, she hadn't had a lot of choice. She couldn't have left him in that hotel room. And what else was she going to do with him? Dump him by the side of the highway?

"We could leave him at the house of a loyalist I know who lives not far off the highway," Henri had suggested. "From there, we could contact the palace and tell them where he could be found."

She sighed. "And have the loyalist arrested for his trouble? I don't think so."

Not only that, but knowing the feelings left over from the war, she didn't trust anyone on either side to do the honorable thing. She wasn't going to let him out of her sight until they found a way to get him back where he belonged.

Of course, this set up quite a dilemma for her. She didn't want to leave Dane alone, and she didn't want to leave her baby alone, and yet she couldn't let Dane know she had the baby with her. She was caught in a balancing act and felt like a tightrope walker whose rope had begun to sway. There had to be some resolution—fast!

Rising from the dressing table in her third-floor bedroom, she turned to look at where Dane lay on her bed, still under the effects of the tranquilizer. Henri had tied his legs together at the ankles and then bound his wrists and tied them above his head to a bolt he'd put in the wall behind the bed.

She hated to see that. She'd stood beside Henri the whole time he'd worked on it, urging him to be careful. But she knew the man was right when he insisted Dane had to be restrained somehow. Still, this was terrible. He was a prince. How could they treat him like this? Right now, she just wanted this whole thing to be over.

Moving closer, she looked down at him, checking his breathing as she'd done every few moments since they'd left the Lion's Mane. He still seemed to be doing all right. She touched the pulse at the side of his neck and nodded. There was no sign of distress in his vitals.

Her face softened as she studied him. His eyes were shadowed darkly, but his color was good and his face was as beautiful as ever. Her smile was bittersweet. What right did he have to be so gorgeous? It wasn't fair.

Memories flooded back, pictures of how she'd found him that last month of the war, barely alive, in the flooded ditch behind the warehouse on her family's horse farm in the hills of Carnethia. She'd dragged him out of his smashed vehicle and into the stables and found a place with sweet, clean straw where she could keep him without others knowing.

She remembered every detail of that night, how he'd lain there where she'd hidden him, wounded and unconscious. She'd done her best, with her simple, rudimentary medical training, to clean out his wounds and sanitize them, to stop the bleeding and make him as comfortable as possible.

She didn't dare tell anyone he was there. The Nationals were rapidly losing the war and they were frantic. They would have killed him with relish. She didn't even dare go for medical help. The few doctors left on the National side were already overworked. Besides, emotions were running high and there was no guarantee that they wouldn't have killed him either.

So she'd been alone, working on hope and whatever she could remember from her training, scared to death she would somehow blot out the flicker that remained of his life. But that hadn't happened, and her ministrations seemed to have been enough. He was alive today.

She remembered the fear she'd lived with, how she'd watched over him, checking his wounds for signs of infection, nursing him through his fever. And hiding him from her family and the servants. It wasn't until the third night that she began to hope he might not die after all.

And then he woke up, stronger than she could have expected he would be. The rest of what happened had seemed like a dream, even then. Somehow, they'd come together, and her baby had been conceived.

Remembering that now, she looked at him. He was still unconscious. His shirt was half-open, the buttons undone. Had those awful wounds healed? Moving slowly, she reached out, slipping her hand under the loose fabric and running it lightly down his chest. Everything she could see looked good and seemed tight and smooth.

She indulged in letting her hand take in the magic of his form for a few seconds. Her heart began to pound. Taking in a quick breath, she pulled away, but at the same time, she glanced up at his face and gasped. His eyes were wide-open, watching her. She jerked her hand away, flushing with chagrin.

"Enjoy yourself," he muttered gruffly, giving a tug to his bonds and wincing at the effort to talk. "But when you're finished, I wish you'd tell me what the hell is going on."

"I was just checking…" she began guiltily. Her voice faded as she realized she had nothing to add. Her cheeks were bright with embarrassment, but she was determined to ignore all that. She frowned at him, lifting her chin.

"As to what's going on, I think that's pretty self-evident. We've got you tied up."

That didn't sound good. She traced her lower lip nervously with her tongue. She wished she could reassure him: *This is just for now. We'll be letting you go as soon as possible.* But she couldn't do that. He had to see her as strong and resolute.

"Be cooperative and you won't get hurt," she said instead, then turned away and grimaced.

"Are you insane?" he demanded angrily, glaring up at her. "This is kidnapping. You can go to prison for this."

"No." But she knew he was right. A dull panic was beating just under her radar, but she couldn't let it surface. "Listen, we had to do this. We couldn't leave you there in the hotel. I…we were worried that someone might do something."

"Like shoot me with a tranquilizer dart?" he broke in scornfully. "Hey, too late. I think that's already been done."

"Dane, listen…."

But he wasn't about to do that. Instead, he wrenched viciously at his bonds, cold anger in his face, swearing a blue streak as he yanked and twisted on the bed.

"Dane, stop it! You're going to pull your arms right out of their sockets," she cried, standing just out of reach and feeling helpless. "Stop and think. You're not a wild beast who beats itself senseless against the bars of its cage. This will get you nowhere."

He paused, breathing raggedly. Sweat glistened on his skin and a trickle of blood made a trail down his forearm. He'd only managed to tighten the cord that held him, but it hardly mattered.

He'd made this ridiculous display out of

frustration and anger. He'd never actually expected it to help him get away. Whoever had tied him up had done a fairly professional job of it. The man knew his knots. It was going to take brains and cunning to get himself released. And that would take a bit of time.

"Dane, we only did what we had to do." She rushed on before he had a chance to dispute that. "If you can stay calm, we'll get through this. We're working on finding a way to release you to your people. But it will take a little more time."

He pulled on the rope that held his wrists. There was anger in his eyes. How could there not be? And yet, he was now calm, watchful.

"Tell you what, Alex. Cut this damn cord and all will be forgiven. Deal?"

"Sorry."

And she really was. She just hated this. Her gaze fell on his wrists, torn raw by his actions, and she winced. "You'll have to stay that way for now. But it shouldn't be for much longer."

He glanced around the room, checking it out. Was he actually tied up in her bedroom?

Or was he dreaming? The whole situation felt surreal.

"So what's the game plan, Alex?" he asked her icily.

She stood over him, hands on her hips, determined not to let him box her into a corner. He was framing this as all her fault. Well, in a way it was, but still, he had something to do with it. She hadn't exactly invited him to drop in at four in the morning.

"You tell me," she said with spirit. "And while you're at it, can you explain just exactly why you had to get in the way this morning?"

He frowned, his dark brows lowering. "You know why. I wanted to talk to you."

She sighed, looking down at him with troubled eyes.

"We can't talk, Dane. Not anymore. What we have to do is negotiate. Don't you see that? Like two huge ships trying to pass each other in narrow straits."

"That's ridiculous." He dismissed it out of hand, looking around. "How did you get me here, anyway?"

"I had help." She sank into a chair beside

the bed. "And luckily, we managed to evade your security detail."

His gaze came back to meet hers. "What security detail? I didn't have one. I came alone to find you."

She stared at him. She could hardly believe that. After the war and all both sides had been through, it seemed illogical at best. "Why would you do something so irresponsible? Who do you think you are?"

He searched her eyes, then laughed softly, though the laughter had a bitter edge.

"Alexandra, I wanted to talk to you. Just you. Not your advisors or guards or brothers. You. Man to woman." He paused, then added softly, "Lover to lover."

"Oh, Dane." Closing her eyes, she turned her face away.

Watching her, he shook his head. "Where are we?"

She looked back at him and wondered what she'd been thinking to bring him here. She'd sent the rest of her entourage to Paris to stay with the community of exiles from the war who had gathered there. That was where her brothers were living and where their father was getting hospital care. She pretended to be traveling by train to Amsterdam, but instead she'd come to stay anonymously in the top two floors of a row house in Triade, a country town about fifty miles to the south. She would have good protection there. The building was owned by an old comrade of her father's who was completely loyal and trustworthy. He would make sure no one knew she was there. She and her prisoner.

"I can't tell you that," she said to Dane.

"Of course not." His gaze hardened. "More to the point, where's the baby?"

She stared into his eyes for a long, long moment, then rose and headed for the door.

"Where are you going?" he called after her.

She whirled, frowning at him. "I'm going to see if I can't find a way to send you home more quickly," she told him. "Isn't that what you want?"

"No," he told her frankly with another hard yank at the rope that held him. "I want to see the baby and I want to see it now."

"Dane!" Marching back, she glared down at him. "You are hardly in the position to be giving orders. We're not in Carnethia. You're not royalty here. You're just a prisoner. So get used to it."

Without another word, she turned on her heel and left, closing the door behind her.

Looking around the room again, Dane let off a string of obscenities. He'd fallen into a trap one more time. Hard to believe that someone so skilled and well trained could let this happen.

But he knew why. He'd let Alexandra bewitch him again. You'd think he'd learn, but no. Every time he was near her he should be prepared to be betrayed—by his own emotions as much as by her.

So here he was, caught in a web. The place was a relatively pleasant torture chamber—even if it was uncomfortable being tied up like this. He'd been in worse. The room was beautiful and sumptuously furnished, with elaborately carved Victorian furniture, thick Persian rugs and heavy draperies that were pulled tightly over the windows.

He had no idea where they were on the map but he was sure this wasn't still the Lion's

Mane Hotel in Darnam. He would have to be sharp, pay attention to every little detail if he wanted to figure out where this was.

He groaned again, angry with her, angry with himself. How lame was this? How had he let this happen? He'd prided himself on being cool, calm and collected. That was what had kept him alive during the recent war. If this story ever got out, he might as well abdicate the throne and let his brother Nico take over.

But that wasn't going to happen. He was going to figure out a way to get out of here soon enough.

Ordinarily he could count on his personal security force to come riding in with backup for him. The trouble was, they had no idea where he'd gone this morning. He'd slipped out without telling anyone. Though they knew he'd gone to Chic's the night before, he hadn't let anyone know he was going to try to catch Alexandra at the Lion's Mane.

In truth, he hadn't wanted anyone to know. He hadn't wanted any interference. He didn't want his actions linked with any sort of official agenda. A private one-on-one with Alexandra was what he'd been after. He had to admit to himself that he'd been hoping for something more…something a bit more intimate.

Well, he was going to pay for that stupid mistake. One of many.

And now, God only knew where the hell he was. So how were his men supposed to find him?

The short answer was, they weren't. He was going to get himself free on his own. But no matter what, he wasn't going to leave without his child.

His child. The concept was becoming more and more real to him now. Everything Alex did confirmed it. The look in her eyes told him all he needed to know. She had indeed given birth to a baby, and that baby was his. The very thought took his breath away.

After all, what had the war been about if not to take back Carnethia for his children? Once he had them. Then had come the fear that he might never have children, that injuries from the war had made it impossible. And now…

He heard the door open.

"I'm back," Alex said, marching in with a

look of clear determination on her pretty face. "I thought I might as well let you know what's going on."

"Why not?" he said, twisting to look at her speculatively. She began to try to use a damp cloth she'd brought with her to clean the raw spots on his skin. He pulled away impatiently.

"Go ahead. Give me the big picture."

"Henri is out contacting some people he knows," she said, shrugging before she dropped the cloth onto the nightstand. "He's negotiating terms for your release right now. It won't be long."

She said it so sunnily, he could tell she really believed it, and that almost made him smile.

"Good," he said, though he wasn't so optimistic as she. "Who's Henri?"

She looked surprised. "Don't you remember Henri? He's my assistant."

He nodded, the corners of his mouth turned slightly down. "Was he by any chance the tall bloke behind the tranquilizer gun?"

She looked pained. "Uh…yes, he was. He was only doing that to protect me, you know," she added hurriedly.

He raised an eyebrow. "And that's supposed to make me feel better about things?"

She grimaced regretfully. "No, I suppose not. Still, you can understand why he felt he had to put a man like you out of commission, can't you?"

"Not really." He grunted, trying to shift his position. He thought he probably did remember Henri from the week he spent in Alex's barn. Part of his foggy memories involved a tall man driving him to a safehouse where his own men came and took him on to the palace. He'd been in extreme pain most of the time and groggy from whatever he'd been given to try to deal with it. But that memory seemed to hold up.

More importantly, did his vague and misty memories of a woman who looked a lot like Alex leaning over him hold up as well? Hard to say.

Looking up, he searched her eyes. "Alex, has anyone told you and your trusty assistant that the war is over? This sort of thing isn't done in civilized society. It's called a criminal offense."

She looked at him for a moment, ready to

argue, but as he watched, her argument melted away.

"I know," she said instead, sinking into the chair and leaning toward him, looking almost apologetic. "Believe me, I can hardly wait to get rid of you." She shook her head. "I just don't know how we're going to do it yet."

He looked at her speculatively, but something told him she wasn't ready to risk untying him. Not yet.

"Is there anything in the news?" he asked instead. "Does anyone know I'm missing?"

She started to say something, then seemed to realize what she was doing. "I'm not going to tell you things like that."

He grimaced. "Why not?"

"You're the captive. I should keep you in the dark about the outside world."

"Why?"

She hesitated. "To you keep you off balance, of course. Because any little piece of information might help you do something I don't want you to do."

He shrugged his shoulders and shook his head, at a loss. "Like what?"

"Will you stop with the questions?" she

cried, frowning down at him. "I'm starting to feel like I'm taking part in that O. Henry story, 'The Ransom of Red Chief.'"

"You are." Despite everything, he found himself letting his wide mouth quirk into something resembling a smile as he stared up at her. "I'm going to do my best to drive you crazy."

The tiniest of smiles was softening her face, too. "Will Carnethia end up making me pay to get them to take you back?"

"Could be. My brother Nico can be a hard-ass at times. He's a pretty tough negotiator."

His gaze held hers for a beat longer than it should have. Something snapped between them, some extraordinary surge of a warm and shivering emotion. Catching her breath, she looked away.

"Remember Tokyo?" he said softly. "How many times did we make love that weekend?"

She gasped, then shook her head with new determination. "I don't remember."

"I do. I remember every single time." He let his gaze drop and caress the soft skin of her neckline, the throb of her pulse at the base of her throat, the way her hair lay in great curls against her collarbone. She was beautiful and memorable and like no other woman in the world.

"I remember exactly how you felt, how you smelled, the way your body…"

"Stop!"

She meant it as an order, but it came out a little too much like a plea, and she colored.

"What if a child had resulted back then?" he asked her, watching her and enjoying the way she reacted so viscerally to everything he said. "What would you have done?"

She raised a trembling hand to push back her hair. "We used protection and nothing happened."

"Nothing happened?" he scoffed. "A war broke out."

She shot him a look. "That wasn't our fault."

"Wasn't it?" he said softly. "As I remember it, the earth moved that night."

She stared at him, shaking her head. "What are you trying to do, Dane?"

His gaze hardened. "I want you to remember. I want you to face the facts. We fell in something very close to love in Tokyo. It might have developed into a lifelong commitment if it hadn't been for the war."

He could tell by the look in her eyes that she agreed with that.

"But it was killed, nipped in the bud. And now a relationship between the two of us is impossible."

"Yes." Her voice was low as a whisper.

"Still, something happened when you found me near your summer home that last month of the war. It still isn't clear to me exactly what, but you know what it was." He gave her a chance to say something, but she was silent. "And since you had a baby nine months later," he went on, "I have to assume we made love."

She made a choking sound but no words came out.

"Tell me the truth, Alexandra," he said, holding her gaze with his own. "That baby you had five months ago is mine, isn't it?"

CHAPTER FOUR

ALEXANDRA held her baby close and murmured loving nonsense into his downy-soft ear as he cooed and looked up at her with huge blue eyes. She took in the scent of fresh-washed baby and sighed.

How she loved this child. What she felt for him was so far above anything she'd ever known. She hadn't realized a woman could love another human this way, so fierce and deep and primal. Her baby was more than a part of her. He was her hope, her dreams, her goodness—everything that was fine about her was wrapped up in a plump pink package of wonderfulness.

Maybe a few of her faults were mixed in as well, but those wouldn't surface until later. Right now all was perfection.

And then there was the Dane part of him. She groaned. She did still have feelings for the man. There was no denying it. That was her cross to bear. She knew instinctively that she would never be happy with any other man. He was the one.

And yet, she could never have him.

How had this happened? How had that one weekend encounter in Tokyo evolved into something so overwhelming? And then it had been cemented into permanence by the week she cared for him at the end of the war. And sealed forever with the birth of a child.

If only…. Oh, if only….

But never mind that. The situation was as it was, and she would have to deal with it this way. There was no use in moping.

Grace, the nanny, came into the room. Alex looked up and smiled. The girl was young and pretty but seemed very reliable. She wore her shiny brown hair in a short bob and every move signaled efficiency.

"You know, Grace, we need to be ready to leave at a moment's notice," she warned her.

"Where will we go?"

Alex hesitated. "I'm not sure yet, but I'm

afraid it will be a long way from here. Do you have a problem with that?"

The girl shook her head. "No, miss. I don't have any family to speak of. When I came to work for you, I promised to devote my life to you and the baby." She looked up, her eyes shining with sincerity. "I meant that promise."

Alex's own eyes stung with unshed tears, surprising her. Reaching out, she took the girl's hand and smiled at her.

"Thank you, Grace," she said softly. "I can't tell you how I appreciate your help."

Grace smiled back, then looked uncertain. "Will we be taking the crown prince with us again?" she asked.

"No." Alex dropped her hand and rose, pulling herself together. "It will be just you, me and Henri. And the baby."

Then she stopped and looked hard at the girl. She hadn't realized Grace understood who Dane was. She knew she'd never mentioned it. But then, if the girl read the tabloids, she might have recognized him on her own. Still…

Truth to tell, she didn't trust anyone right now. There was too much hard feeling in the air, the sort of resentment the losers always had against the winners. She didn't even dare leave him alone with Henri, though she knew her assistant was wily enough to know the danger inherent in letting anything happen to Carnethia's crown prince. He wasn't sense-lessly filled with threats of revenge like her brothers were. And then there was Kavon. She wasn't sure. The way he'd looked at Dane, she felt he wasn't to be trusted.

Still, what did a wary look mean? Not much.

There were those among her people who hated Dane the way her brothers did. Bitterness and war could twist men into doing things they wouldn't ordinarily dream of doing. She'd seen that in her brothers and she knew to be careful.

If Marque and Ivan knew she had Dane captured like this, she was terrified to think what they might try to do. The feeling between the two families was rancid and fraught with ugliness. She didn't dare leave him until she'd figured out what in the world she was going to do to safely get rid of him.

Sighing, she turned away. She was sure

Grace was all right. She'd been recommended by Gregor Narna, the doctor she'd been using since Robbie was born and she'd worked out beautifully.

She was sick of being so suspicious of everyone around her. It would be a relief to travel halfway around the world to a place where Carnethia was almost unknown.

"He's getting sleepy," she told the girl. "I'm going to feed him and put him down for a nap. Why don't you go and get some rest while you have the chance."

Grace nodded and left the room, and Alex settled down to nurse her baby. Whatever else happened, she had this bond that meant so much to her. Softly she began to sing a lullaby, but her mind was racing with apprehension.

Dane had been working on the knots that held his hands. He was going to get them untied. All it took was patience and time. But he could only work on it for so long and then he had to rest for a bit. He was a little groggy, still feeling the effects from the tranquilizer dose he'd received that morning.

Once he had his hands free he would have

to move carefully, scoping out the situation and seeing what could be done. He had to figure out how many people she had here with her. And whether they had weapons.

Besides the tranquilizer gun.

He dozed for a few minutes, then jolted awake to what he thought was a baby's cry. But no matter how hard he listened, he couldn't hear anything. He must have been dreaming. He had visions of babies dancing through his head, even in his sleep.

Relentless, he went back to working at the rope. He'd escaped from tougher bonds before. He knew a few tricks but nothing seemed to be working.

"Damn," he cursed in flinty frustration.

At the same moment Alex came back into the room.

He looked up, feeling like growling, but her unusually disheveled appearance, with her shirt open an extra button down, made him forget his anger. Despite everything, she was a pleasure to look at.

"Would you like a drink of water?" she offered, holding out a cup toward him.

He was suddenly very thirsty, especially if

it meant having her come close enough to touch.

"Why not?" he allowed, then waited as she sank down onto the bed beside where he lay.

He lifted his head and she carefully held the cup to his lips, keeping an eye on him to make sure he could take it in without spilling.

Watching him drink, a wave of tenderness came over her. It was something akin to the way she felt about her baby, and yet so very different at the same time. Her gaze skittered over him, looking for familiar things—the crease in his ear, the crinkles around his eyes, the silver scar on his neck. She'd always loved the way his hair came to a widow's peak.

She wished she could run her hands through that auburn mane, flexing her fingers, pulling his face to hers, kissing those hard, warm lips with a hunger that had built up for years. She'd done it before, but that had been a long, long time ago.

How she'd missed him. The feeling surged in her chest making it hard to breathe.

He was drinking slowly, enjoying the sense of her so close. He liked the look of the casually open shirt with the glimpse it gave of her creamy breasts. He pretty much liked everything about her. But suddenly it hit him like a flash from heaven and his head jerked back away from the cup.

She'd been breastfeeding his baby. The baby was here.

He closed his eyes as the realization sank in, not even hearing what she was saying as she took the cup away. He didn't want her to see his reaction and realize he knew the baby was in the building. A strange, anticipatory joy filled him. His soul sang. His baby was here. Finally he was going to see him.

It was peculiar that he cared so much. Until fairly recently, he'd hardly given it a thought. But with all this nonsense about there being some evidence that he might not be able to have any more children because of injuries and his fever during the war, he'd begun to realize the subject was a big one. And when he'd heard that Alex might have had a child, puzzle pieces had begun to fall into place.

Alex, the only woman he'd ever come close to loving, had given birth to his baby. It was too much to take in all at once. Opening his eyes, he stared at her in wonder.

"I've heard from Henri," she was saying. "He says we should be able to get you back to your people by nightfall."

"What?" He blinked up at her, his heart still full from thinking about his baby. "Run that by me again. I wasn't listening."

She sighed with exasperation, but did as he asked. "Henri called. He's in contact with Count Rodigan."

Dane nodded. "A good man."

"I hope you're right, because he's doing the negotiating. If he's an honest broker, we'll soon be rid of you. Thank God."

"Why Alex, I'm shocked," he mocked lightly. "But you know you'll miss me when I'm gone."

"Not likely." She tossed her hair, her green eyes flashing. "Henri will know what's best. He's the one who got you back to your people that last time, so…" Her voice trailed off as she realized she was admitting something she'd avoided talking about before.

"The last time." He stared at her, his blue eyes intense. "You mean that last month of the war, don't you? So you admit it. You did take care of me."

She sighed. "Yes, I did take care of you. I thought you were remembering all that on your own."

He nodded. "Little by little, a lot of it is coming back to me, but in misty, dreamlike sequences. I still can't quite make sense of it all." He gazed at her speculatively. "How did you find me?"

She stared at him but what she saw in her mind was a confused picture of the tangled wreckage of his military vehicle at the bottom of the drainage ditch and the panic she was in as she tried to pull him out of it and drag him up to her barn. He'd been bleeding badly, from knife wounds as well as the crash. She'd been so afraid he would die. And she hadn't dared go for help.

And now it was very different in that he wasn't losing blood and near death. But here she was, still afraid of what people from her side might do to him. It was a dangerous and ridiculous situation and she wasn't sure how she had let it develop to this stage.

The solution to all the short-term problems was getting rid of Dane without him coming across proof about the baby. That was the first priority. He thought he knew the truth, but she hadn't let him have the satisfaction of admitting it.

Right now he was suspicious, but he didn't have the goods. She had to get rid of him before he let his dreams become reality. Let him wonder. Keep him off balance.

She laughed shortly, shaking her head. If only she could. He was the one who was tied up, so why did she feel like the captive? Instead of answering him, she began to pace the floor, her arms folded over her chest.

"Here's what I don't get, Alex," he was saying, still watching for her reaction. "Why am I here?"

"What?" She turned to look down at him.

"You are obviously not holding me for ransom. You don't seem to be after any sort of revenge." He paused, then added coolly, "Unfortunately, there aren't any signs you want me around for long nights of debauchery."

"Hardly," she said with a shudder.

His eyes narrowed. "So what's it all about, Alex?" He waited a moment, and when she went on pacing without answering, he added, "Where are your brothers right now?"

She stopped and looked back at him again. "What does that have to do with anything?"

"I'd just like to know. Is Ivan involved in this?"

The look on her face told him volumes.

"Are you serious?" she said. "It's because I wanted to make sure Ivan didn't find you that I insisted we bring you here."

He raised an eyebrow. "So you know that your brother is threatening to kill me?"

She'd heard all right. Her eyes didn't lie.

Turning away, she began to pace again. "He thinks you left him to bleed to death."

Dane closed his eyes, nodding. "I did."

He heard her gasp softly and then she was standing right over him, staring down.

"No, you didn't," she said forcefully.

His eyes narrowed thoughtfully as he looked up at her, bemused but interested. "How do you know?"

She stared at him. Should she tell him the truth? Why not?

"Because I was there. Well, not during the fight, but just after it."

"Fascinating. Care to enlighten me?"

She shook her head, but then she sighed and sank down to sit beside him on the bed.

"Okay, here's how it looked to me. I was by myself out in the paddock at the summer farm that day, training a new horse, and I heard a car coming down the mountain. It was crashing through the brush, completely out of control, and I heard it smash into the drainage ditch. I ran over as fast as I could, afraid anyone in the car might drown. And there you were, half hanging out of an army vehicle."

She took a deep breath as memories swept over her. "You were a mess. Blood was everywhere."

He studied her face, wondering if he could believe her. His impulse was to ask for some backup for her story, but he resisted. It did fit into the scenario that was beginning to build in his mind's eye. He remembered being wounded, hardly able to function, but trying to drive down the mountain, anyway. And then things got fuzzy.

"Quite a coincidence, eh?" he said instead.

She shook her head, staring at the wall, letting the memories flow. "I could hardly believe it. There you were, the one man in the world I—"

She stopped herself and glanced at him quickly, cleared her throat and went on.

"And when you opened your eyes and looked up at me, you said…" She stopped again, frowning. Maybe it would be better to skip this part.

"What did I say?"

She sighed. In for a penny, in for a pound. Why not be honest? She gazed at him levelly as she told him.

"You said, 'Alex, is that really you? Am I dreaming? Or am I dead and this is heaven?'"

He laughed shortly. That sounded right. That was exactly how he would have felt at finding the one woman he'd ever cared for saving him from drowning in a ditch.

"I don't remember any of that," he said candidly. "How long did I stay with you?"

She rose and turned away. "Long enough to become quite a nuisance," she said coolly. "Henri found someone who could come and get you and then you were gone."

He was quiet for a moment, thinking that over, and then he said, "How strange that you've done something to put me in the same situation again, in a way. Don't you find that odd? This is pretty much a replay of that incident."

"Not exactly." She turned back to look at him. "But close. Still, this time we have to take you to a neutral position. We can't let anyone know where this place is. That makes it harder."

He stared at her. Strange, but he was completely confident that he would be able to free himself before Henri and his vaunted negotiating got involved. He had no doubt he would be going home soon. And his child would be with him. He was pretty sure that hadn't been part of her plan when she'd decided to kidnap him.

But maybe if he analyzed what had happened over a year ago at her family's summer farm, he would gain some insights.

"I remember something of that day," he said slowly. "I remember going up to Kerstin Castle."

She nodded. "So it seems. That was where you were coming from."

"I came face-to-face with your brother Ivan up there. We fought."

She went very still. "Yes."

He frowned, thinking back and remembering things he hadn't thought of for months.

The war had hit a turning point about then. Things were going well. The Nationals were retreating everywhere, leaving behind areas his family's supporters hadn't been in for fifty years. When Dane got word that Kerstin Castle had been evacuated by the enemy, he couldn't stay away. The castle was legendary, the site of the birth of the house of Montenevada, the place where his ancestors ruled from during the sixteenth century.

He'd grabbed an armored vehicle, a French VBL, and tore through the countryside until he saw the castle high up on Kerstin Mountain. He made a cautious approach, just in case reports were premature, but there was no sign of anyone on the road up the mountainside, no sign of anyone in the parking area outside the castle walls, no sign of life, period. He pulled the vehicle over to the side and hopped out, entering carefully.

Once inside the gates a sense of reverence

for the past, a wave of awe, a surge of deep emotion, all combined to overwhelm him. As he made his way over stone floors, he could almost feel the presence of his ancestors, hear them calling down the hallways. The feeling of being a part of his country's history was all around him. He ran up the marble staircase, marveling at the ancient beauty all around him, and then he turned a corner and found himself face-to-face with Ivan.

Like a fool, he'd left his weapon outside. Ivan hadn't been so stupid. He was pointing a gun right at Dane's face. With a strangled obscenity, he fired. Or tried to.

Dane was certain when he thought of it later, that his ancestors had taken a hand in what happened. The gun jammed. Cursing, Ivan tried again. And again. And finally, he threw the gun at Dane as he charged him, reaching for the knife he wore at his hip.

Dane got to him before he had a chance to use the knife effectively, grabbed him, and they both went down, rolling and wrestling for the weapon. The blade went into Dane's chest once, then again, but he didn't feel it.

Everything in him was focused on getting the knife out of Ivan's hands. He got stabbed once more before he succeeded, but at last he had control.

He was bleeding badly, but he had the knife.

"Get back," he'd yelled at Ivan, stumbling back himself.

Ivan charged him again, yelling as he came, and this time the knife went into Ivan's neck. With a groan, Ivan slumped to the cold stone floor. Dane stared down at him for a moment, but he wasn't moving.

Turning away, he staggered out and struggled into the vehicle. He was hurt and bleeding all over the place. His one thought was to find help. He began to drive, taking turns at random, struggling to stay conscious. As he came down the mountain, going faster and faster, he saw a large farm ahead, and that was the last he remembered.

It was amazing they had both survived that day.

"And now Ivan's spreading the story that I left him there to bleed his life away." He frowned. He'd done that, he supposed, but only because Ivan had wounded him so badly, he couldn't do much else. "What do you know about that?"

She pressed her lips together before she answered. "I know that Henri went up to the castle and found him there and he had medical help fairly soon," she said softly. She looked at him. "You were bleeding badly, too. It was obvious the two of you had tried to finish each other off."

He nodded. That about told the story. Then he looked at her, one eyebrow raised. "If things happened the way you say they did, you saved my life."

"Did I?" she said, a hint of sarcasm in her tone. "Was it worth it?"

He grinned lopsidedly. "*I* think so."

She turned away.

"Was there a price to pay for saving me, Alex?" he asked softly. "Did you have problems because of it?"

She turned back, looking defiant. "What I do is my business. I don't do anything I don't want to do."

"Or have a good reason for."

"Exactly."

He nodded. "So tell me, Alex. What was your good reason for bringing me here?"

She drew in her breath. "Can't you guess?"

He shrugged. "I don't know. I might be useful for something. I suppose you could keep me on hand as your personal sex slave. That's one thought."

She shook her head at his ego. "Dream on, Your Highness. I don't think you're quite suited for that role."

He widened his eyes innocently. "Try me."

Her mouth quirked in one corner and she did look a bit amused. "You're tied up."

"Yes. And you say you never do anything without a good reason."

She threw up her hands. "Oh, for heaven's sake!"

"I think you should kiss me at least."

Beyond all reason, she had to laugh at that. "What?"

He nodded like a man with new insight, his eyes crinkling at the corners. "And here I never realized I might be able to get into this bondage stuff."

She suppressed her smile. He was so appealing. He had the look of a man who needed a shave, and somehow that made him even more attractive. "Don't be ridiculous."

"I'm not. You should kiss me while you've got the chance."

"Why?"

He shrugged. "So you can say you did. When are you likely to have another captive you want to make out with?"

She was caught by his gaze and she just couldn't look away. Her heart was beating faster. "Who says I want to make out with you?"

He smiled, giving her heart another adrenaline surge. "Your eyes say it."

"No they don't." But she turned her head away just to make sure.

"Liar." His voice was husky, another provocative element he'd added in, just for the fun of it. "What are you so scared of? I'm tied here. I can't do a thing to you."

She shook her head.

"Consider it torture," he suggested.

"How can kissing be torture?" she scoffed.

"It'll be torture to me," he said softly, "because I can't touch you."

She drew in her breath. "Dane…" she said warningly.

"Oh, come on, Alex, kiss me," he coaxed.

"No." But she wasn't moving away, was she?

"Alex…" His voice deepened and darkened. "Every part of me yearns for you. I've been yearning for you for six years. Take pity. Give me a crumb."

She looked down at him, her own longing in her eyes. How often had she obsessed about Tokyo, how many nights had she lain awake recreating that weekend in her mind?

"Oh, Dane," she sighed, "if only…"

"Kiss me."

Looking down at him, she was tempted. What could it hurt? Dropping to sit beside him on the bed, she leaned down slowly, barely touching her lips to his. He closed his eyes and took in her scent, the feel of her hair sweeping over him, the warmth of her body, so close and yet so far away.

"Alex," he began, his voice tortured.

"Hush." She sat up straight, listening intently. "Someone's here."

CHAPTER FIVE

DANE lifted his head. Alex was right. Voices.

"Someone's here," she said again, pressing her hand over her heart as she listened, her breath coming faster.

Dane frowned. He didn't like the look on her face.

"Henri?" he guessed hopefully.

"No." She met his gaze. "Ivan."

He swore softly, knowing this wasn't good without her having to explain it to him.

"How did he know we came here?" she muttered fretfully as she rose from the bed. "I thought I laid out a pretty good red herring toward Amsterdam." She shook her head, looking down at Dane with troubled eyes. "You stay still," she ordered, starting toward the door.

But before she reached it, she stopped and

turned back. Dane watched as she moved quickly, dragging a large wooden screen out across the floor into the center of the room and opening it fully, shielding the view of the bed from anyone who might get as far as her bedroom door, effectively dividing the room in two.

It was frustratingly annoying to be lying here, helpless, with Ivan in the building. Dane frowned and bit down on his lower lip, hard. This was not good. He'd run into Alex's brothers before and every episode had left a bad taste. That last encounter at Kerstin Castle had led to Ivan supposedly regaling many a dinner party with tales of different methods he might use to exact his revenge on the crown prince of Carnethia. He hated to think this set up a perfect opportunity for the man.

Dane had stabbed him all right, but not in the way he was claiming. And Dane would be happy to tell him so, face-to-face. But now wasn't exactly a convenient time for it. He was at something of a disadvantage.

Even more important, he was here to find his child, not to get bogged down in trying to settle old disputes. He would just as soon avoid having Ivan know he was here. So he wasn't against her putting up the screen. However, there were better ways of dealing with this.

"Maybe you should release me," he suggested quietly.

She glanced at him. "I wish I could," she murmured, then hurried toward the exit again.

The door opened before she reached it. Though Dane could hear what was happening, the screen shielded any view he might have had of the scene.

"There you are," a voice said. It certainly sounded like Ivan. "What are you doing up here?"

Alex sounded flustered. "I...I was just—"

"Well, never mind that. I can't stay long. I just stopped in to say hello and to find out what happened."

"What happened?" Alex was regaining her balance but her voice was still a little stressed. "What do you mean?" she said quickly. "Nothing happened."

Ivan sniffed. "I heard Dane showed up at the club last night, at Chic's."

"Oh. Yes, he did."

"And?"

Dane could hear her trying to get to the doorway. "I'll tell you later."

Ivan obviously stopped her. "Later? I told you, I don't have much time."

"Ivan, let's go downstairs. It's more comfortable."

"No, that idiot Kavon is hanging around down there. I don't want him listening in to our conversation." Dane could hear a chair scraping across the floor. "Let's sit down here. I've only got a moment."

It sounded as though they both had sat in chairs. Dane began working at the bindings that held him. He didn't relish lying here like a lamb to be slaughtered should young Ivan decide to come around the screen.

He had no problem with confrontation. He could stand his ground well enough—once he was upright at any rate. Gritting his teeth, he forced his mind to concentrate on finding a way to release the knots. If Ivan started to roam, there wasn't going to be a lot of time to spare.

"Wouldn't you like to go downstairs and get something to eat?" Alex was saying brightly.

It almost made him grin to hear how determined she was to get Ivan back down the stairs. Ivan, however, had other plans.

"Alex, relax. Why are you so edgy? I'm fine right here."

She moved fretfully. "But I'm not. I want to go downstairs."

"You still haven't told me what happened when you saw Dane at the club," Ivan was saying. "Did you talk to him?"

"Yes." She turned back to look at him, feeling sulky now. Funny how being with her brothers always seemed to make her act like a child again. Those old patterns died hard.

"Well? What did he say?"

She stared at him, wondering what he wanted to know. "Nothing that would interest you."

Ivan's face twisted. "Lover's secrets?" he probed in a sarcastic tone.

Alex sat a little taller and lifted her chin.

"Don't try to goad me, Ivan," she said with a certain regal dignity. "I don't care enough to fall for your tricks."

Dane was still working at the knots that held him, but he heard every word, and listening reminded him just how deep his fascination with Alex went. She was a pure mixture of womanly nobility and girlish charm. He was never sure which face she would show him at any given time. Her emotions ran close to the surface and she couldn't hide her reactions, even when she wanted to.

But she could put on the deep freeze when she felt it necessary. And her brother was feeling some of that chill right now.

He supposed that was part of what drew him to her. She was different from any woman he'd ever known.

Females had begun throwing themselves at him by the time he was fourteen. He'd taken it for granted as long as he could remember. Someone had once said that power was the ultimate aphrodisiac, and he was an heir to the sort of power that fit that picture.

But she hadn't responded that way in Tokyo. As a matter of fact, for once he'd had to be the hunter. And when he'd finally captured her and trapped her in his bed, he'd been shocked to find this gorgeous, sensual woman was still a virgin.

That shouldn't have made any difference, and yet…it did. It made what had happened in Tokyo special—the most special encounter he'd ever had with a woman.

It was a memory he cherished, just as he cherished recalling the way she'd smelled, the way her hair had spread out before him on the white pillows, the way her skin had seemed to glow with desire for him that weekend.

Yes, it made her more special, and at the same time it made him feel more guilty. He hadn't meant to love her and leave her the way he had.

Parting from her in Tokyo had been excruciating. He boarded his flight for home certain he had found the woman of his dreams. How he was going to convince his father he wasn't sure. But he knew he would. Only one thing could come between him and his hopes.

The war began within hours of his return home. At first it seemed only a dramatic show of strength to firm up bargaining positions. But before long it was a full-blown invasion. And once his father had filled him in on all the battle plans, he'd known his relationship with Alexandra was over.

That had been six long years ago. He'd changed a lot since then. So had she. But from what he'd seen at the club, and now here, she was more beautiful and desirable than before. And also, completely out of his reach forever.

But she'd had his baby. He was convinced of that now, and everything about this situation was only making him more so. His baby was here and he was going to find him.

"How did you know I was here?" Alex was asking her brother.

"I didn't. I thought I'd take a chance and it paid off."

"Where's Marque?"

"He's gone back to Paris to check on Father." Ivan's voice hardened. "You should go to see him, you know."

Alex sighed. "There's not much point. He won't let me into his hospital room."

"Well, yes. He refuses to see you until you put that baby up for adoption."

Dane went stock-still. This was new. He'd always known Alex's father was a hard man—men who took over countries usually were—but this seemed a bit radical, even for him. The man wouldn't even accept his own grandchild?

"I'll never do that." Alex's voice was firm, brooking no retreat.

"It's your duty." Ivan sounded somewhat bored with it all, but just as adamant as his sister.

"My duty!"

"Yes. If we are going to gather the strength to fight the good fight to get Carnethia back in our grasp we have to form a united front. One for all and all for one, just like before. We can't have a suspect baby hanging around."

"A suspect baby! Oh!" Alex sounded as though she would cheerfully throttle her brother at this point.

"You know damn well Father can't accept the little bloke. We all know where you got him."

"Shut up, Ivan!"

"Should I just go ahead and say it?" Ivan continued, sounding as supercilious as Dane had always thought him to be.

Alex rose from her chair so energetically, it crashed over behind her. "No! Let's take this downstairs, Ivan. Come on."

"No, Alex. I'll just say it. Everybody knows that bastard Dane Montenevada is the only man you've ever let into your bed."

"Nobody knows anything," she cried, furious. Her hands were clenched into fists at her side. She didn't want to hear this, didn't want Dane to hear it.

"Are you denying it? That baby is a Montenevada. I'm still not sure how the bastard got to you, but it must have been right around the time I had my run-in with him. Was that it? Did he think he could get his revenge by dropping in to impregnate you right after trying to kill me? Was that his game?"

"Ivan, you don't know what you're talking about." Her voice was so cold it dripped icicles and she just barely resisted taking a swing at his smug face.

"Maybe not, but I still say he's a traitor baby. And part of the Montenevadas' campaign against us. Father won't see you until you do something about it. It's for the larger cause."

"The larger cause," she repeated with infinite scorn. "The larger fantasy, you mean."

"See?" He threw up his hands. "How do you expect Father to forgive you when you say things like that? You have no respect for our family honor. You have no faith in the fight. You aren't part of the united front."

"Oh really? So how is that going, that united front?" She was mocking him now. "Got lots of recruits, do you? Molding men into soldiers? Ready to march on back in and take the palace?"

Ivan was pained. "You know it's kind of slow right now. It'll take some time to build momentum again."

"Exactly." She kicked at the fallen chair, anger in every movement she made. "It's never going to happen and you know it. You need someone with will and charisma to pull that off. The sort of man our father was once upon a time. He's too old and sick, and you and Marque just aren't quite…"

Her voice trailed off. Despite her rage, she didn't want to hurt him unnecessarily. But he should face facts.

"Yeah, well, you're just proving why you don't seem like one of us anymore," he said dismissively.

"Oh, Ivan!" She turned and closed her eyes, holding back her fury.

"Wait a minute." Ivan's attention had been caught by something else. "Hold on. Why do you have this screen up? You never had it there before."

She whirled, looking at it and blanched. "I…listen, Ivan, it's none of your business how I set up my bedroom."

He rose, staring at the screen. She stepped forward and stood in his way.

"What are you doing?" he demanded, glaring at her. "Why are you standing there as though you're trying to block my way into your room?" He reached out to give her a shove, but she wouldn't budge. "What are you hiding?"

"Nothing," she said, her green eyes flashing with anger, her heart in her throat. "I'm not hiding anything. I require a bit of privacy, Ivan. You have no right—"

"Let me see."

Once he'd put his mind to it, he pushed past her easily, striding into the center of the room.

She leaped forward, prepared to throw

herself on Dane's body if she had to. But the bed was empty.

She stopped and stared at it, then looked wildly about the room, before she thought to cover up her reaction. There was no sign of Dane anywhere. Even the rope that had held him was gone, though the bolt was still plainly visible in the wall.

Luckily, Ivan was still swiveling and staring around into corners as though he thought he was going to catch her with something illicit, and he didn't seem to notice her relief.

"Nothing," he said, disappointed. "Hey, you should import a lover or two. That would at least be a little interesting." He glanced at her pale face. "But you're only interested in one lover. I know, I know. The man who cut me and left me to bleed to death. Some sister you are." He smirked at her. "Maybe I should use you as bait to get him where I want him. Believe me, someday I'll make him pay for what he did to me."

"Look, you can stay here if you want," she retorted haughtily. "I'm going downstairs."

He grinned at her. "So am I. I need something to eat before I take off. You going to fix me something?"

She sighed, letting him go out the door first, then looked back and wondered where in the world Dane was hiding. "All right," she said. "I think Kavon picked up some meat at the market. I'll make you a sandwich. But only if you promise to go away and leave me alone once you've eaten."

"Sure," he called back over his shoulder. "Right after I take a short nap. All this arguing has tired me out."

Her sigh was even more heartfelt this time. One last puzzled glance at her empty room and she was on her way downstairs.

CHAPTER SIX

GRACE entered the baby's room on the second floor, yawning as she came in. She'd been napping but she knew it was past time to check on young Robbie. When she saw the crown prince holding the child, she gasped and reached out to catch herself from falling over.

"Oh!" she cried, then dropped into a deep curtsy. "Your Highness," she said, and when she looked up her eyes were shining.

Dane barely glanced at her. He'd finally pulled the bindings that were holding him captive loose and made his way into Alex's closet, crouching there while he waited for them to leave the room. He'd heard everything and knew now, without a doubt, that this baby was his. As soon as the path was clear, he'd made his way down a floor and begun to search through rooms. He'd found the baby in the second room he entered.

He'd gone straight to the crib and then stopped, stunned by the emotion that was choking his throat. His hands were shaking and he curled his fingers around the bars of the crib while he looked down and saw his child for the first time. The beauty of the little face, the tiny fingers, the downy sprinkling of hair, the rounded cheeks, all combined to create a sense of holiness and magic, all at once. His breath caught in his throat. He was almost afraid to touch him.

But he did, and once he'd let his hand cup the warm head, let his fingers touch the tiny chin, watched as the big blue eyes opened and gazed at him, he'd felt a chuckle of happiness building in his chest. He'd reached for the child, pulling him carefully up into his arms and holding him as though he'd been doing this forever.

His child. He closed his eyes in a quick, silent prayer of joy.

That was when Grace entered the room. He noted her reaction, though his attention was mostly focused on Robbie. Who would have guessed the nanny would be an instant ally? Something was deeply suspicious here, but he didn't know what and he didn't have time to mull it over. His baby was in his arms.

"What do you call him?" he asked her.

"Robbie. Short for Robert James."

He nodded, looking bemused. "Is he a good baby?"

Her smile lit up the room. "The best. You're going to love him."

He looked at her, surprised again. But he knew she spoke the truth. "I'll look after him for a while," he said, dismissing her.

"Of course, Your Highness," she said. "I'll be in the next room if you need me."

"Thank you."

She paused. "Your Highness, one more thing, if I may."

"Yes?"

"If you need the car brought around, I have a certain amount of influence over Kavon, the attendant downstairs. I can make sure it happens."

He nodded, looking at her with a touch of wonder. One surprise after another with this one.

"Good," he said. "Why don't you do that, then?" He frowned, remembering there was more to this situation that needed to be dealt with. "Can you manage it without letting Ivan know?"

"I think so." She looked at him with bright eyes. "I'll do my best."

"Great. Thank you very much."

She nodded, seeming pleased. She left quietly, but Dane had forgotten her already. His mind, his heart, his soul was on this child he held in his arms.

There was no doubt the baby was his. He saw it in every inch of baby flesh. He gazed down at the huge blue eyes watching him and his heart swelled and choked in his throat. Tears filled his eyes. What before had been a need on a theoretical basis became concrete and real. The bond he felt with this baby was immediate and complete. He had to have his child with him. Nothing could get in the way of that.

And Alexandra? A sense of icy chill shadowed his joy. He couldn't deny he saw a lot of her in this baby as well. He knew without seeing it that her heart and soul were bound up in this child's welfare. How could he take her baby from her? It seemed impossible. But even more impossible was the thought of leaving him behind.

Closing his eyes, he took in the magical sense of life in his arms, the baby smells, the firm, plump feel of that perfect body, the tiny bubbling sounds, and his heart overflowed.

His baby. His future. His life.

He heard Alex as she rushed up the stairs. He'd known she would come right away with plans to hide Robbie from him somehow. But he'd made his way to the nursery too quickly and she was out of luck. He heard her at the door and he didn't look up.

Her sigh sounded like heartbreak. She took in the scene and knew what this meant.

"So you've seen him," she said, moving in closer. "You know."

"Yes."

"But it doesn't matter," she went on fiercely. "No court in the world will take him away from me."

He finally looked up into her eyes and found them full of tragedy. He didn't let her see evidence of the feeling that sliced through him at the sight. She was beautiful, even in her agony. And she was the mother of his child. His heart went out to her, but he couldn't let her know that. Not yet.

"We'll see."

His tone froze her heart. He was firm, confident. A stone wall. He had no intention of listening to reason.

What could she do? Ivan was still downstairs, lying down on the couch to catch a little sleep before moving on. She could run down, wake him…and what? Set the two men off against each other while she tried to pull her baby out of the middle of the fight? No. There had to be a better way.

She glanced at Robbie in the prince's arms, and her heart stopped. The baby looked so right with him, gazing up sleepily and reaching a chubby hand toward his face.

"Dane, you wouldn't be this cruel," she said hollowly.

He drew in a sharp breath. "Alex, I heard everything your brother said. I understand how all this is tearing apart your relationship with your father. And here, I've got the answer to all your problems." He threw her a serious look, searching her eyes, wondering if this had occurred to her. "I'll take the baby with me and you can go back into the bosom of your family."

She winced, a spasm of horror at the concept. "No!"

"I'm sorry, Alex."

She shook her head, emphatic. "You can't take him. I have to feed him."

He hesitated only a second or two, and then his expression lightened, as though he'd had an epiphany. "Then you'll have to come along."

She stared at him, amazed he was even suggesting it. "Impossible."

He met her gaze and held it for a long, long moment. Then, unexpectedly, he reached out and cupped her cheek with the palm of his hand, and a speculative expression crept into his gaze.

"Nothing is impossible, Alex," he said, his voice showing evidence that he had just realized this himself. "You can come and stay in the palace until he's weaned."

She reached up to pull his hand away, but somehow her hand stayed there, covering his. What he was saying made a certain sort of sense, and his gesture should have meant a feeling of warmth toward her. But his eyes were still so hard, she didn't trust it.

"Like a servant?" she said, her voice breaking as she fought to hold back tears. "Like a wet nurse?"

He searched her eyes. "If you characterize it that way, you'll come as a combatant. I'd rather you came as a partner. You have to understand that this isn't up for discussion. I'm taking him. It's up to you whether or not you come along."

She finally pulled away from his touch, grimacing.

"This is crazy, like something from medieval times."

"We all do what we have to do, Alex. I've had to adjust. So will you."

She tried to think things through, but her mind was racing and panic kept flaring in her heart. Swinging around, she stared at him, her palms up. "What are we talking about? You can't do this." She twisted with pain. "You won't get custody. They won't take a baby from his mother."

He shrugged. "I'm afraid you're wrong about that. Where royalty is concerned, direct line of descent is more important to most people than mere mother love."

"But...but he's born out of wedlock."

He nodded. "True. If I wanted to disavow him, I probably could. But I don't. I'm going to claim him as my own, my direct heir. No one will dispute that."

"We'll see about that."

He shook his head, looking at her with barely concealed sympathy. "You have no power base behind you any longer. I've got a whole country. The courts and everything."

"I've got fairness," she insisted, knowing she was beginning to sound desperate. And why not? Desperate was exactly what she was. "I've got what's right on my side."

"That doesn't go far in the world we live in, Alex. Power is the bottom line. And you know very well how it is. You and your family once had it and you used it to your own advantage at the time." He shrugged. "Now I've got it. Like I said, you're going to have to adjust."

She closed her eyes against the hot tears

that threatened, knowing she was beaten. The succession of kings was everything, wasn't it? She should have known from the beginning she would never be allowed to get away with having her own baby. Not when that baby was going to be a crown prince in his own right.

A dark wave of resignation came over her. She was going to have to face the inevitable. She couldn't call upon her family to defend her. They wouldn't lift a finger to help her keep Robbie.

She thought quickly. The first thing to think of was her baby's well-being. Crown Prince Dane wanted Robbie. He wanted to do well by him. She didn't think for a moment that he would do anything to hurt him. Her only real option was to go along.

"Okay, Dane," she muttered more to herself than to him, swaying with agony. "You win. But you don't get Robbie without me."

He nodded, his bright gaze sweeping over her. Actually, that prospect made his heart soar. Didn't she know how much he'd adored her six years ago? The pain he'd lived with when he knew he had to give up all hope for their relationship? He didn't expect to take up where they'd left off, of course, but he cared about her more than any other woman he knew—except, perhaps, his sister, Carla.

"So be it," he said, wishing he could comfort her. But this wasn't the time. They still had things to do, including managing to get out of here without alerting Ivan.

Turning, he pulled a blanket up to wrap Robbie in. "If you have anything you want to take along, bring it quickly," he said. "I want to get out of here."

She left the room, running up the stairs to her own bedroom, and he forced himself to slow down and think things through before he made his next move. He had his baby. He had the nanny on his side, a car and a supposedly willing driver.

Even Alex was committed to going along, if only to protect her child. He admired her for that. It looked like there were only two stumbling blocks to watch out for—Henri, the man with the great big tranquilizer dart gun, and Ivan, the man who wanted him dead. Seemed like it would be a brilliant plan to avoid them both.

Alex came back into the room, and Grace

appeared, as well. She went up to Alex and put a comforting hand on her arm. "It'll be all right, miss," she whispered. "I'll be there to help you."

Alex looked at her blankly. She was moving in a fog, not sure what people were saying to her, nor why.

"Is there a back stairway?" Dane asked Grace.

"Yes. Come this way."

Grace led them down to the ground floor. Dane was carrying the baby. Alex trailed along as though she were going to her doom. She had a vaguely uncomfortable feeling that Grace seemed awfully calm, and then a moment of surprise to see that Kavon had pulled the car up to the back door and seemed ready to drive them to Carnethia. This was all a bit convenient for Dane, wasn't it? Should she point this out? Raise some questions? Maybe not yet. But she filed away her reactions to mull over at a later time.

She got into the back seat of the huge car and so did Grace. Dane put the baby in the carrier and strapped him in between them. Just as he straightened in order to get into the front passenger's seat, Alex and Grace both gasped, and he turned quickly to see Ivan coming around the corner. The two men froze as they faced each other.

"What the hell?" Ivan growled, then looked around quickly for something to use as a weapon.

Dane beat him to the punch—literally. Stepping forward, he caught him with an upper cut to the jaw. Ivan went out like a light and Dane hopped into the car.

"Step on it," he ordered Kavon, who reacted with satisfying speed. "Head for the border." He sighed, looking back at his sleeping baby. "We're going home."

The drive seemed endless. Dane stared out the window at the passing landscape, but his mind was churning with what he'd done, what he had to do. He was going to be crowned king of his country very soon. That brought with it certain responsibilities, and one of the most important was to have a child. Succession mattered.

He was going to have to find a woman to be his queen. A king needed a queen. It was part of the ruling structure, and he was prepared to do his duty. But he knew that whatever woman he chose, it would be a pure business arrangement. She would be perfect for the job but she could never be perfect for his heart.

Alexandra Acredonna had stolen his heart six years ago and she'd never given it back. Looking at her now, he wondered if she understood that. But it hardly mattered. There were emotions deeper and more important than love. Hatred was one of them. So was revenge. Destiny had decided to make it impossible for the two of them to be together the way they would have liked. Too bad.

Time would tell how this would end. But at least he had his son.

They were still a few hours out when night fell.

"Are you hungry?" Dane asked, looking back at Alex.

She shook her head. She still felt as though she were in shock. Her every expectation had been stood on its head. Just earlier that same day, she'd kidnapped Dane. Now he was returning the favor. Her mind was flashing from one thought, one emotion, to another, and she wasn't sure how to stop that.

"I haven't had anything all day," he noted. "There's a little country inn up ahead. We can get something there."

By now they were inside the boundaries of his country and had added a police escort. As they pulled into the parking lot, people turned and stared, but Dane was behind tinted glass and they couldn't see who it was that was causing the commotion. Kavon and Grace went in to get some light food for take-out, leaving Alex and Dane in the car with the baby.

Dane turned and watched as she took Robbie into her arms and sang to him softly.

"Do you hate me for doing this?" he asked her softly.

Her green eyes flashed defiance as she met his gaze. "I don't know if *hate* is actually a strong enough word," she returned.

But she was lying. And as she looked at him, she knew it. He probably knew it, too. She was angry, yes. Disappointed, resentful and scared.

But she didn't hate him. How could she when she saw the expression in his eyes as he gazed at their baby? He already loved

Robbie just as much as she did. That meant there was a bond between them that could never be completely severed. Like it or not, the three of them were family—of a sort.

"Don't you see that there was no other way?" he asked her.

She supposed, from his point of view, that was right. But for her…

"No other way than to destroy my life?" she asked, trying to make her tone light and lose the bitterness.

"Your life is pretty much your baby at this point, isn't it?"

Yes, but she wasn't about to admit it to him. "I do have friends," she protested.

"Friends…and lovers?" He used a casual tone, but it was clear he was very curious about the answer to that one.

"I've had a few men of interest in my life," she said defensively as she made some adjustments to the blankets around the sleeping baby. She knew he'd heard her brother accusing her of wanting no man in her bed but the crown prince, and Ivan had certainly hit the nail on the head. But she wasn't going to admit it to Dane. Not for a moment.

"Ah, yes," he was saying wryly. "Men such as that jerk you were dancing with last night."

She turned to look at him, startled. "Which jerk?"

He laughed shortly. "You know who I mean. The one who acted like he had a right to touch you." It was obvious that fact still rankled with him.

She shrugged. "I have so many male friends," she said airily.

His brows drew together. "The tall one with the silver at his temples. Overweening dignity. Basically a pompous ass."

She was aghast. "That wasn't a pompous ass. That was Jarrod. He used to be our foreign minister."

Dane's mouth twisted. "There you go."

She pressed her lips together to hold back the trace of a smile. "Don't you remember Jarrod? Surely you met him in the old days."

He frowned. "Ah, yes, I think I do vaguely remember the man. He tends to linger on the mind, sort of like an oil slick that you can't get rid of."

She rolled her eyes. "He's a very nice man and he wants to marry me."

He groaned. "I knew I would find reason to hate him."

She shook her head, exasperated with him. "What do you care? You don't want to marry me."

"I don't want to marry anyone." He paused for a moment, then added as he gazed at Robbie, "But I do want my child."

She sighed. "But you see, that's not the way it usually works. You are supposed to woo the lady of your choice, marry her and then come the babies."

"Too clichéd." He smiled at her in the moonlight. "We seem to have skipped a step."

"Yes." She said it softly, meeting his eyes and feeling a connection that was becoming too familiar. "But that step wasn't an option for us."

"True. Do you regret that?"

She didn't answer. They didn't have much more time before the others returned with the food, and she had something else she wanted to talk to him about. It was a very touchy subject and she wasn't sure she had the nerve to deal with it. But in some ways she had to.

"Is it true what the tabloids say?" she challenged him bluntly at last.

"Almost never. Don't read them."

She bit her lip, wondering if she really wanted to get into this. But why not? One thing she was resolved to do was to speak her mind, no matter how angry it made him. If they didn't have truth between them, this situation could get out of hand very rapidly.

"I don't usually," she responded to his suggestion that she not read the tabloids. "But I couldn't avoid seeing stories about you over the last few months."

He looked wary. "And?"

"You know what I'm talking about."

He waited, one eyebrow raised with something approaching disdain, and she sighed and prepared to continue. He was going to make her do this the hard way, wasn't he?

"Okay, here it is in a nutshell. They've been writing that your injuries from the war, and the fever you had while recuperating, have left you—" words failed her for a moment, but she blinked and forced herself on "—unable to have children."

He didn't flinch and he didn't explode in anger as she'd expected. He just nodded and said, "I've heard those same rumors."

"Well? Is it true?"

He gave her a sardonic look. "There's nothing wrong with my performance, if that's what you're worried about."

She flushed. "I understand that infertility is not the same thing as impotence," she snapped. "And I'm asking again, is it true?"

She waited, heart beating a fast rhythm in her chest. Suddenly the answer seemed very important. And the way Dane was procrastinating made it seem even more so.

He turned away, staring out through the windshield. She waited, wondering if she was going to get any answer at all.

"Well, I'll tell you, Alex," he said slowly at last. "I haven't tried to propagate any new members of the species lately. So I can't give you a definitive answer to that question."

She shook her head, puzzled. "Can't you be tested?"

"I could if I wanted to be. But I don't."

"You don't want to know?"

He turned back and his wide mouth

twisted into something very near a smile. "I don't need to know. I have my child."

Alex's breath caught in her throat, but Grace and Kavon were back with the food and she couldn't go on with the subject. The more she thought about it the more she realized the truth of his medical situation made all the difference in the world to them both—and to their son. If Dane could never have another biological child, Robbie's position was secure. But what of her own?

She'd read the tabloids, just like everybody else. She'd been chilled by the rumors of his secret baby because she knew he did indeed have one. But when she'd heard the deeper, darker rumors that he would never be able to have other children because of lingering injuries from the war, she'd been skeptical. After all, he'd fathered her baby while he was recovering.

Of course, she didn't know what might have happened to him after Henri got him safely back to his own people. She'd heard he'd had a terrible fever. There was no telling what that meant. But that was why there had been such a frenzy to find his secret baby—

possibly the only heir to the throne that he would ever have.

Now he'd found his child. What next?

An hour later, as they entered the outskirts of the capital city, Dane turned back to speak to her again.

"We'll go directly to Altamere," he said, naming the royal palace. "I called my sister, Carla. She'll be getting things ready to receive us."

"Very good," she replied. "You know, I've met your sister. Before you and I knew each other, I knew her."

He looked surprised. "Where was that?"

"In Vienna. At an international conference on antique dolls."

He almost laughed. "What?"

"It was a hobby of mine years ago. And your sister was into it, too, at the time. We got along fine once we got past the usual suspicions. We made a pact right from the beginning to ignore all that and just have a good time, and we did. As a matter of fact, we were partners in a couple of workshops."

He shook his head. "It's a small world,

isn't it?" he said softly, taking in how she looked in the moonlight and loving it.

She nodded, wishing for just a moment that they were alone in the car. There were times when she looked at him that the old feelings came back so strongly, she almost choked on them. A strong pull of attraction still existed between them. Too bad. That very fact was going to make things more difficult than they needed to be.

They arrived at the palace before midnight. Alex began to feel chills as soon as they entered the city, and when the spires of Altamere appeared ahead, she could hardly breathe. It had been more than a year since she'd seen the home she'd grown up in, the beautiful palace and grounds that had been the base for her family for half a century. It felt very strange to be returning under these circumstances.

"Like a hostage," she thought sadly. "Like the last remnant of a conquered tribe."

They came in through a side entrance. Her heels struck sharply on the marble floor, echoing through the elaborately decorated hallways. The tapestries, the oil portraits of ancient Carnethian kings, the plush upholstery, all looked familiar and comforting.

She remembered the way the place had filled with warmth and happiness on holidays when her mother was still alive. Her brothers had been like playful puppies in those days. Even her father had seemed more kindly. Her eyes stung. What her family had lost.

And now she was here as the enemy. She wasn't sure how the others of Dane's family were going to treat her. Would they even accept her presence here? Maybe not. Maybe someone, one of the princes, or an old uncle, or someone—would start shouting when he saw her.

"Out! Out! We'll have no Acredonnas here, with their vile cheating ways and their false promises."

She half expected it, and when Dane came up beside her, she swayed, wishing she could tuck her arm into the crook of his and come in under his protection.

"You okay?" he asked, looking down at her.

She nodded, determined to keep a stiff

upper lip. Then a voice came down from the top of the stairs.

"Welcome, Alexandra."

She turned to see pretty, dark-haired Princess Carla coming down the wide staircase. Her smile was genuine and she held out her hands for Alex's.

"I'm so glad you've come to stay with us," she said, her face shining radiantly. "We've already got Mychale's baby, Brianna, who's about the same age as yours. And Nico's wife, Marisa, is about to have her baby any day now. And with your little one, we'll have a full set."

"Thank you for being so kind," Alex said, her voice shaking a bit.

If Carla kept being such a sweetheart, she was going to have to cry. That wasn't how she wanted her first evening at the palace to go.

But it was wonderful that the princess of the Montenevada family could be so kind to a daughter of the Acredonnas, the people who had cast her family out of Carnethia. Was the woman an angel, or was she hiding her true feelings? Hard to tell. And Alex was too tired to make heads or tails of it, anyway. She was just grateful for a friendly face.

The princess oohed and aahed over Robbie for a few minutes, endearing herself even further into Alex's heart, and then turned back to her brother.

"I had the rooms you requested set up for them," she said, giving Dane a look. "But are you sure they are really what you want? The east wing hasn't been used in decades. It is so off the beaten path around here."

Dane's hard face brooked no argument. "That's exactly what we want," he said shortly. "At least until things get settled and we decide how this is going to work."

His gaze skimmed briefly over Alex's tired face.

"The less fuss the better. We want to keep this quiet as long as we can. The fewer people who know, the more chance we have to keep this out of the papers."

Carla shook her head. "They always ferret things out," she warned. "You can't stop it."

"No," Dane agreed. "But we can make it as hard for them as possible."

Carla shrugged. "As you wish, brother dear." She smiled at Alex. "Come along. I'll show you to your rooms."

CHAPTER SEVEN

TRUE to his plans, Dane installed them in the east wing. Alex had grown up in this palace. It had been her home until the Montenevadas had changed all that. But even she had hardly ever been in the east wing. Most of the rooms had been closed when she lived there.

The fact that Dane picked that location to store them away in spoke volumes to her. In fact, he hadn't tried to hide his intentions. He wanted her and her baby as far out of the limelight as possible.

Still, the room he'd picked out for Robbie was large and beautifully furnished. Very soon it was full of baby toys and baby furniture. An entire staff of servants was at the ready, including an assistant for Grace.

Her baby was treated as royalty. And why not? That was exactly what he was.

She herself had a small room off the main nursery, and Grace had the same on the other side. So far, no one had tried to hinder her access to her son. She was sure she could come and go at will.

But she had no idea what was going to happen when Robbie was weaned. Was Dane going to expect her to disappear? Was she going to be allowed to see him on special holidays only? Just how much of a part was she going to have in raising her own child?

But that was all a long way off. Time enough later to think about what she would do when the strains and hurdles of living here in a Montenevada enclave became everyday problems for her.

She was leaning over the beautiful royal crib in the midmorning sunlight when Dane arrived for his first visit.

"Morning," he said shortly without looking at her. Instead, he leaned over the crib, too, and smiled down at his child. "How's my big boy this morning?" he murmured, more to the baby than to her.

But she answered anyway. "He seems to be fine."

"Good. Hi, Robbie. Hi, big guy."

Despite everything, his tone made her smile. It was nice to have someone else around who enjoyed the unique qualities of this baby as much as she did. Straightening, she looked at Dane in a way to draw his attention away from playing with the child.

"I have a favor to ask," she said, managing a cool exterior. She didn't want to put herself in the position of begging, but there were things that needed to be attended to.

"What's that?" he responded, looking up reluctantly.

"I'd like to get in touch with Robbie's doctor and have him come by to give him a quick checkup. After the way we've carted him all over the country these last few days, I'd just like to be sure."

"Of course." He nodded, his eyes hooded but not unfriendly. "I'll have my secretary take care of that. What's his name?"

"Dr. Gregor Narna."

Dane did a double take, then stared at her.

"What did you say that name was?" he asked, incredulous.

"Gregor Narna."

Dane frowned. "I know that name."

"Do you?" She dangled a rattle over Robbie's happy face and laughed as he reached for it, then sobered quickly. "I'm not surprised. He's quite an expert in the royal family's health matters."

"Yes. Yes, he is." Dane still stared at her curiously. "How did you end up with him?"

She shrugged. "He and my brother were friends during Marque's short-lived stint in medical school. I heard about his royalty specialization—I don't remember where—and got in touch with him just before Robbie was born."

"Ah." He understood now. Of course. She knew she was going to need someone who had worked with the Montenevadas before, as her baby carried the royal family genes with all their quirks and eccentricities.

He had mixed feelings about that. On the one hand, it made his heart swell with pride to be reminded the boy was really his. On the other hand, he resented those months of preparation for Robbie's birth that he'd missed out on. And then there were the first five months of his baby's life. Why hadn't she let him know?

Resolved: he wasn't going to miss another minute he didn't have to.

"I thought Narna had been having trouble getting fully credentialed as a physician," he said. "Something about his eyesight being injured in the war."

"As I understand it, he got that straightened out just recently. He can't do surgery, but he can see patients privately."

"Well, I'm glad you had the foresight to hire him," he said a bit stiffly, watching her leaning over the child and thinking she was even more beautiful as a mother than she was as a lover.

Dressed in a flowing red morning dress of some sort of silky material with her glorious hair swirling around her face and her shoulders, she looked sexy and exotic and very much like she ought to be the royalty here. But he was going to have to stifle those sorts of thoughts, wasn't he?

"Yes, he's been wonderful." She pulled the

blanket up over Robbie's pudgy legs. He wasted no time in kicking it back off again. "He's the one who found Grace for me, too. And she's been the perfect nanny."

"Has she?" he said softly, remembering how quickly the girl had seemed to come to his side at the hideout house the day before. It was almost as though she'd just been there, waiting for him to free himself so that she could spring into action and help him escape. And what if that really was the case?

He had to turn away to hide a smile. More and more of that picture was becoming clear to him. He wondered who was behind it all. Something told him his sister might know the answer to that question.

"There's just one more thing." She looked up at him, hesitated, then lifted her chin and went on resolutely. "What about Henri? Could I have him here?"

He almost laughed aloud at that one. "Are you crazy? The man attacked me with a dart gun."

"He only did that because he thought he had to protect me," she said earnestly. "He's been my right hand since I was a child. I really feel lost without him."

"Sorry, Alex." He shook his head. "I don't think we can risk having your personal guard dog prowling around in the nooks and crannies of the palace, looking out for your interests."

"But you've allowed Kavon to stay. And Grace. Why do you trust them so much?"

"Maybe because they haven't tried to attack me."

"But…they haven't been put in that position, have they? Not like Henri was."

"Are you saying they would be attacking me in some way if only they had the chance to?"

"No. Of course not. But I still don't see why you accept them so easily when you don't accept Henri."

"Why not? They're good people."

"Yes, but…they work for me."

He just smiled and it chilled her heart. She had visions of herself all alone with no one on her side. She didn't like that much.

"Listen, Alex," he went on, once he'd decided to try to explain. "Kavon is so crazy about Grace, he'll do anything to stay near her. Besides, he's a gun for hire. Henri is devoted to you and you alone. That's quite a different matter."

She hated this. She wasn't used to having to beg, borrow and steal to survive. She was accustomed, in fact, to pretty much getting what she wanted when she wanted it, war or no war. Was she going to have to learn to get the things she wanted by subterfuge? How rotten that would be.

But she managed to leash her resentment and hold her request for a later review. After all, there would be a lot of things she would have to adjust to here. Might as well hold off on her demands until she could prioritize a little better.

He turned and flashed her a wary gaze. "I'm having you watched, you know."

She gave a short laugh. "How could I miss it? I've practically got a target on my back."

His mouth tilted in a slight smile. He was glad he'd told her up-front. He was learning that honesty could often be hard, but it paid off in the end. He didn't want any secrets between them. This entire situation was going to be hard enough to deal with without that.

"It's annoying, I know. But it's necessary. I can't take the chance that you'll grab Robbie and bolt."

"If only," she muttered darkly.

Reaching out, he took her chin in his hand and forced her to look up into his face.

"Do you get that, Alex? Do you see that I don't take this lightly?"

She searched his eyes for a moment. They were fierce with an inner strength she could only envy.

"Yes, I understand all that. But you needn't worry. I don't have anywhere to run to, do I?"

He shook his head. "There's always someplace."

She stared at him and for the first time all day, she began to feel her fighting spirit stirring again. Reaching up, she pressed her lips together and pushed his hand away.

"I'm not a nobody," she insisted, getting tough. "I'm not a little girl off the street you can have total control over."

"I know that, Alex." He shrugged. "But you are the enemy."

The enemy. She drew her breath in

sharply. If she was going to be that the whole time she lived here, there was no hope for normal life, was there?

"No." She shook her head so hard, her hair whipped from one side to the other. "The war is over. No more enemies."

He winced as though her emotions were too bright to look at head-on. "You're dreaming, Alex. What about your family? They aren't ready to give up the fight. They don't believe in letting bygones be bygones. They don't buy it. Why should I?"

She sighed, shoulders slumping. "The rest of my family are the ones living in dreamland. I'm a realist. I'm ready to let the war go." She made herself look into his eyes again. She had to know if he realized what she was saying to him. "I can move on. It's hard, but I can do it. In fact, I have to. I have a child. I can't live in the past."

What she saw in his gaze made her heart sink. Something in him wanted to reach out to her—maybe even halfway. But he couldn't. He wasn't ready. He couldn't quite summon the will to put the war and all it entailed behind him.

As she moved—terrified—into the future, she was on her own.

"On the other hand," she said lightly, hoping he couldn't see that her heart was breaking, just a little bit. "I can adjust to circumstances. Don't let me get in the way of your eternal struggle against whatever. I'll just cheer from the sidelines, if you don't mind."

"Yes," he said, his tone just as casual. "But which side will you be cheering for? That's the question."

Robbie began to fuss and she turned away from Dane while she tended to him. When she turned back, the crown prince was gone.

Dane was back late in the afternoon. She was looking up remedies for cradle cap when he appeared in the doorway. He nodded stiffly toward where she sat in the window seat and walked straight over to the crib to see his child.

"Would you like me to go and leave you alone with him?" she asked, starting to gather her things for departure.

He looked at her, surprised.

"No," he said. "I won't be here long."

She inclined her head. "As you wish."

Putting her things back down, she waited as he murmured sweet nonsense to Robbie for another few minutes.

He was dressed as though he'd just come from a business meeting, all stiff white collar and sleek Italian suit coat. A conventional facade, she thought to herself, over a spectacularly unconventional male form. She rather liked the fact that she knew the hard, muscular body beneath the camouflage in ways not many of his subjects did. It was her little secret.

He came over to where she sat and glanced down at the book in her lap. "Is there a problem?" he asked when he saw what she'd bookmarked.

"Not yet," she told him. "I'm just schooling myself on signs of trouble to look out for."

He nodded. "Dr. Narna is coming tomorrow. Right after lunch."

"Good. Thank you for calling him."

He hesitated and she sat waiting, not saying a thing. She wasn't about to try to make life easier for him.

"Have they brought you enough clothes?"

he asked, glancing at the trim blue sweater and designer jeans she wore. Her wonderful hair was captured in a clasp and propped at the back of her head, leaving her looking slightly bookish.

"Yes. Very nice ones, too." She waved a hand in the air. "I think I'll never have to shop again."

He frowned. "Why the sarcasm? Isn't that a good thing?"

She eyed him balefully. Men. There were some things they just would never understand. "Please."

He waited, but she didn't add anything. She was determined not to smooth over the fact that she was here against her will.

"So, are you comfortable here?" he asked at last.

"Oh, yes," she responded. "For a prison, it's very nice indeed."

"Oh, really? At least you're not bound to a spike in the wall."

She grimaced. "Yes, well…I'm sorry about that. Hadn't I mentioned that before? It was necessary but evil." She shuddered delicately and gave him a tiny, mischievous smile. "And I promise I'll never do it again."

"You'll never get the chance. Once bitten, twice shy."

She shrugged with nonchalance she really didn't feel. "The bigger they are, the harder they fall," she quoted, matching one saying for another.

He started a retort, but caught himself in time and bit his tongue. Beginning to pace, he shoved his hands into his pockets as though to keep from strangling her—at least, that was the way it looked to her.

"So what do you want, Alex? What can I do to smooth your way here? What would make you happy?"

She pushed back loose hair that had come free from the clasp. "You know the answer to that, but we both know it ain't gonna happen."

He stopped before her. "You're never taking Robbie from me, if that's what you mean." He said it as an axiom. No doubts, no arguments.

"That's what I mean." She gave him a fake smile. "Oh, well."

"Alex, Robbie is here for the duration." Set in stone. No doubts. No turning back. He hesitated, then added, "I hope you'll stay, as well."

"Do you?" She searched his eyes. "Why?"

He searched for a response, then seemed to hit upon an answer that would suit. "Because you're his mother. And he ought to have his mother with him."

She nodded slowly. "I don't plan to be parted from him," she agreed. "But at the same time…" She paused, wondering how to put this. After a deep sigh she said, "I'm completely at sea, Dane. I don't know what my place is here. I don't feel right. I don't feel at ease. I have no real status."

When he merely stared at her as though he had no idea what she was talking about, she went on.

"I feel like I'm dancing on eggshells. I'm just not sure where to put my feet."

He shrugged. "You're the mother of the new crown prince, and as such, you have a certain stature no matter what other circumstances apply."

She shook her head, trying to make him understand. "What good is that when I'm here as a prisoner?"

He frowned. "You'll get used to it," he said shortly. "Give it time."

She sighed, exasperated with him. He wasn't about to see this from her vantage point. Didn't he know this was an impossible situation for her to be in? Didn't he realize it was making other things worse—such as relations between her family and his?

She still had her mobile and had been getting reports from people she knew. From what she'd heard, her brothers were already rallying support among the faithful, using the fact that Dane had snatched her and her baby and was now supposedly holding them both prisoner in the palace. She knew such things could only reinforce her father's anger against her.

And that was another thing. Her father lay dying in a hospital room where she should be herself, attending to him. And yet, here she was hundreds of miles away from that.

"Some things aren't going to get better with time," she told him. "Some things just can't wait. For instance, I do want to go see my father. But I can't."

"Because he won't see you?"

"Not only that." In truth, she could probably talk her way in, if her brothers weren't around. "If I left, what guarantee do I have that you would let me back?"

He stared at her. "Is that what's stopping you? You don't trust me at all, do you?"

She looked up at him, her eyes wide. Didn't he get this? "How can I? You've declared that we are still enemies. You hate my family. You took my child."

Anger simmered in him now and he couldn't hide it any longer. "Alex, you are free to go anytime you like. I won't hold you here."

"But you won't let me back, either, will you?"

He hesitated. "All things being equal, I don't see why I wouldn't let you back. But circumstances can change."

"You see?" She threw up her hands and glared at him, her green eyes flashing sparks. "I'll tell you this. If I do go, it will be to find a lawyer to begin proceedings against you. I'll fight you through all the courts of the continent if I have to."

His face darkened and looked harder than she'd ever seen it.

"If that's the way you want to spend your

next few years, be my guest. Believe me, I'll have better lawyers and more money and rigged trials if I have to. You won't win."

She knew he was right. As he turned on his heel and marched from the room, she sighed and started to laugh softly. At least she'd let him know how she felt. And he'd revealed a few things himself. Better to know up-front what you were in for.

Robbie burped and she laughed again.

"Thank you for that considered opinion on the matter," she teased him. "Come on, you baby, you. Time for your bath."

Whatever else, she knew she would never, ever do anything to jeopardize her time with her baby. That was all that really mattered.

There was a note with her breakfast tray the next morning.

"If the weather holds, let's take Robbie out to the stream at ten," it said.

"Let's"? That was a contraction for "let us." She and Dane were an "us"? Who knew?

She sighed. She'd just spent a restless night deciding it would be smart to avoid Dane, to raise her boy as though Dane wasn't a factor in his life or hers, and the first thing that happened was a note from him setting up an expedition and there went her heart, all aflutter.

"'What kind of fool am I?'" she sang to herself as she changed Robbie's diapers.

The worst kind of fool, obviously. For some crazy reason the fight they'd had the day before seemed to have cleared the air in many ways. She felt free and fresh and ready to see him again. Eager in fact. Yes, *fool* was probably the right word for it.

Carla came visiting just as she was clearing away the breakfast dishes.

"Hi," she said cheerfully as she came sailing into the room, a vision in beaded net and textured denim.

From what the others had told her, Carla had lost weight in the last few weeks and now looked almost model slim and definitely gorgeous.

"A sign she's in love," Grace had said with a laugh.

From the look of her, Alex would have to agree.

"I just had to come say hello to the young

prince here." She bent to take his little fingers and let them curl around one of her own. "And to warn you about the St. Tupin's Day Ball," she added with a significant look Alex's way.

Alex shook her head. She vaguely remembered that St. Tupin had been a big deal to the royalty, but that had been before her time, and her family hadn't paid much attention to him.

"Why do I need warning?" she asked warily.

Carla grinned. "Because I'm going to make you go to it."

"Oh, no, I can't possibly."

"Yes, you can. And Dane won't even know you're there."

Alex made a face. "What are you talking about?"

"I've made it into a masquerade. Just for you. Well, and for one other reason." Carla chuckled. "I've got a dress picked out for you and everything. You must come."

"Oh, Carla. I really don't think I should."

"I won't hear any excuses. It's my coming out, at last. And I'll need all my friends around me."

Alex frowned. "Aren't you a little old to be coming out at this late date?" she asked before she thought. "Oh! I mean…"

"Don't worry. I feel the same way. But they're making me do it." Leaning close, she whispered into Alex's ear. "What they don't know is I've invited a few unsuitable friends."

Alex made a face. "Male friends?"

She nodded happily. "So I have to tread carefully." She laughed. "I'm making them come in masks, as well. No one will know."

Alex wasn't so sure she shared Carla's confidence that all would go well with everyone pretending to be someone else. But it wasn't her ball. And once she got over her initial worries, the prospect seemed like a lot of fun.

"I'll do it," she promised. "But only for an hour or so."

"Of course. You have a baby to care for. I understand."

Dane's sister was so warm and friendly, it was hard to turn her down. Thank God there was at least one relative who seemed to like her. When she thought about it she had to wonder at the others. Dane had two brothers, each with wives, and a great-aunt name Lady Julia, a number of uncles and cousins and various other relatives living here. Why was it that the only one who'd made the effort to come and see Robbie—and see Alex, too, for that matter—was Carla? Probably her Acredonna ties were too repellant for the taste of the others.

Well, too bad. They didn't know what they were missing.

CHAPTER EIGHT

AN HOUR later she had Robbie ready for his outing. She'd rummaged through all his brand-new clothes until she found a little blue suit with a knit cap and matching knit booties that suited the occasion. He looked cute as a bug.

Dane thought so, too.

"Every time I see this little guy, he looks more like those babies you see in the soap commercials," he said.

He'd come in with an expectant look, and she'd found herself greeting him with a smile. That seemed to set the tone for their outing. It was as though yesterday's arguments had been filed away and they were on a new blank page. That was fine with her. She hated confrontation, though she never would have admitted it. She'd needed to be tough a lot in her life and she could do it. She just didn't enjoy it as much as others thought she did.

"With a baby this beautiful and this well turned out, we ought to take him to the promenade and show him off to the world," Dane said.

Alex laughed. He was obviously quite serious. She only wished such a thing were possible.

But they did show him off to the birds and the butterflies and the little gray squirrel that hung off a branch and chattered at them.

The stream ran through one corner of the large plot of land the palace stood on. A small forest of shimmering trees had been planted all along the banks and a jogging/hiking trail rolled alongside the water. Once inside the tree line, the city seemed to melt away around them and they were transported to the mountains, in thought if not in reality.

"I always did love it here," Alex told him as they strolled along the path, Robbie in the perambulator. "I spent hours here as a girl."

He nodded. "This has to be my favorite

place in the whole city," he said. "My grand-mother used to tell me about it when I was a boy. When we finally got the palace back, this was the first place I had to see."

"She died without ever seeing it again herself, though," Alex noted mostly to herself, thinking she was lucky that hadn't happened to her.

"Yes. She died long before the war to regain the country."

Alex nodded, realizing that the woman they were talking about was her son's great-grand-mother. The two families were now inextri-cably tied together forever. Dane's parents were her child's grandparents. How strange.

"Your parents didn't get to enjoy the res-toration much, either," she noted.

"Not for long," he agreed. "My father was killed at the very end, and my mother died of a broken heart."

"Oh." Alex winced. "Mothers do that a lot, don't they?"

He didn't answer for another beat or two, and then he turned on her.

"Rubbish," he said, gazing at her, his blue eyes crinkling with amusement. "I don't buy that at all. It's the women who keep us going. You're the strong ones."

He was looking at her as though he thought she was the most beautiful thing he'd ever seen. She could see it in his eyes. She laughed out loud and felt, for a moment, happy to be alive.

They threw pebbles into the stream and found a bird's nest, the broken blue eggshells still inside. Coming upon a nice flat rock, they sat and watched the water, their sleepy baby gurgling beside them.

"Tell me something, Alex," Dane said at last. "After that first weekend in Tokyo—when we met." He glanced at her sideways. "If you'd gotten pregnant and had a baby then, would you have told me?"

She pulled her arms in tight and shivered as a cool breeze swept through. The light linen pantsuit she wore was no defense against an impending cold front.

"I wouldn't have been able to—or allowed to."

He frowned, thinking that over. "You were very much under your father's thumb in those days, weren't you?"

"Of course."

He looked at her. "And now?"

She sighed. "Now he is very sick. Near death."

He frowned. He knew what Ivan had said, but still he wondered. "Why aren't you with him?"

She shivered again. "He's angry with me. He doesn't want me there. Well, I take that back. My brothers have convinced him he doesn't want me there. I think he would speak to me if I went."

"Because of Robbie."

"Yes. But that's only a part of it. He's angry at us all for letting him down. He thinks we didn't do enough to keep your family from taking back the country. He's old and he's bitter."

Looking up, she met his gaze. "I'd like to go see him, but I can't. And my brothers…" She shrugged.

He knew she'd complained about her fears of not being allowed back if she left, but he knew they could work that out and he sensed something larger in her dilemma here. After all, she'd said she was ready to move on from the emotions that had been so hyped by the war. But the others in her family weren't.

And what about him? What was he ready for? He hadn't been able to meet her halfway yesterday. Was he going to change that stand? Was there going to be a thaw in his frozen reactions? If anybody could get him to change, this woman was the one.

A raw sense of affection for her crashed through him like a wave on the ocean. His original feelings for her had been good ones. The more he was with her, the more he knew she was the only woman who could ever hold his heart. The irony was, she was the only woman he could never allow to do that very thing.

As they rose to go back to the palace, he knew he had to tell her how much she meant to him. Despite everything, she had to know. There was no telling what the future would bring. He might not have another chance.

"Alex, wait," he said, his voice husky with emotion.

"Yes?" She turned, raising her face to him in question.

He stared down into her eyes, then groaned

and reached out, taking her by the shoulders and pulling her close. "Alex, I just have to tell you how I feel right now. We can't be together, not the way we would want to. But you've done something for me that no one else could ever do."

"Dane…"

"You've given me the greatest present a woman can give a man," he went on. He shook his head, gazing down into her eyes, his own feeling misty. "He's perfect." He shrugged. "And I just want you to know how much I appreciate it. Thank you."

She smiled up at him, tears in her own eyes. What he'd just done surprised her, but it filled her heart.

"Why not?" she said. "You've given the same to me."

He laughed softly and dropped a light kiss on her lips. She kissed him back. He hadn't expected that. For just a moment they were lost in a tender warmth that felt so wonderful, neither wanted to pull away.

"Alex," he murmured, his hands beginning to slide down her back.

"No." She reached up and pressed a finger

to his lips to stop him from saying anything. He'd said enough and she didn't want him to do anything to ruin it. "We'd better go in."

She felt light as a feather the rest of the day. She knew he still cared about her. And more than anything, she knew she still cared about him. Surely there would be some way to find an answer to their problem. They were the parents of the most important child in their world. They had to do what was best for him.

But what was that? Unfortunately, that wasn't so clear.

Dane arrived late that evening, looking firm but a bit defensive, as though to show what had happened by the stream was a one-time event. He hadn't gone all soft and squishy on her.

He played with Robbie for a few minutes, then came to where Alex sat in the window seat. He stood before her, but there was a sense of restlessness in his vibe and she moved over.

"Sit," she offered.

He looked tempted but shook his head. "I'm not staying," he said. "Did Dr. Narna show up? What did he say?"

"He said Robbie was the picture of health. And the most perfect baby he'd ever seen. And the most beautiful." She smiled. "Or maybe I just thought I heard those last two things. But they're true, nonetheless."

He nodded. "Good." He looked at her, then away, then back again. "Well, I just wanted to let you know you'll be presented to the royal family tomorrow night at dinner in the main dining room."

She froze. She hadn't expected this. She hadn't wanted it. But of course. He had to do something to explain to the rest of them what was going on. It was only logical. Still…

"No," she said, loud and clear, looking up into his face.

"No?" He looked at her, incredulous. "What do you mean, no?"

She lifted her chin and met his gaze resolutely. "I mean I won't be dragged into the dining room to be laughed at and gossiped over by the royal family."

He was so astonished, for a moment, he couldn't speak. "My family would never treat you that way," he said at last. "You have to come. I've told them you're coming."

She waved a hand in the air. "Tell them my plans have changed."

"No, I will not tell them that. You're coming."

He couldn't believe she was being so obstinate. He'd thought she might even be pleased. If she only knew what he'd gone through to get his family to agree to let her come to dinner, she might not be so cavalier about this. His brothers and sister had no problem with it, but some of the older members and a few of the closer counselors were adamantly opposed to her and everything about her. They wanted her gone, and Nigel Rowe, his legal counsel, had prepared all sorts of logical arguments as to why Dane should get rid of her immediately.

"She has no right to be here, Your Highness," he'd cried, the veins in his neck swelling with passion. "You must take complete custody of the baby. I'll draw up the paperwork. Let her see him at Christmas and on his birthday. That's all she needs. You don't want her spreading her foul Acredonna attitudes into his young life. He's got to be raised as a Montenevada through and through."

He'd stood his ground and fought them all to a standstill. He'd ordered Lady Julia to attend the dinner, despite her sudden attack of the vapors at the thought. And he'd laid down the law with the cousins from Belgrade.

"You will all be there," he'd roared at them at last. "Every one of you. And if anyone does the slightest thing to make Alexandra feel unwelcome, you'll pay for it."

There had been some glum faces, but they'd all reluctantly agreed to attend. And now Alex was refusing to come herself.

"You don't have to stay for dinner, if you don't want to," he told her. "All you have to do is allow me to present you, curtsy as though you actually have some manners, smile nicely and then you can leave the room."

She ignored the vague insult as though it were beneath her notice. "It isn't the length of time, Dane. It's the act itself."

He threw up his hands. "Alex, this is ridiculous." He felt anger brewing and he was bound and determined not to let himself blow up over this. Instead, he was going to act smart. He was a bottom-line sort of guy, wasn't he?

Okay. Bottom line. "What will it take to get you to do this?"

She stared at him for a long moment, gathering her courage. She'd thought long and hard about this and she knew what she wanted.

"I can tell you this," she said, holding his gaze with her own. "The only way I will allow you to present me to your entire family is—" she swallowed hard "—is if I'm introduced in an official capacity."

His head went back. He wasn't sure what she meant. "Such as?"

"Such as…" She gulped in a big, sustaining breath and went on, talking very quickly. "Such as your future wife, for instance."

His jaw dropped. "What?"

"Yes, that's it." She raised her chin defiantly. "Marry me, Dane."

He stared at her, shaking his head, his eyes dark as shadows. "You know that's impossible."

That was a stab to the heart, but she barely stuttered, saying, "Yes, I do."

His face could have been chiseled from granite. "Why bring it up, then?"

"To establish some parameters."

She was angry now and she couldn't hide it.

"If you can't find a way to marry the mother of your son, I think you'd better get to work figuring something else out. I won't be treated like the spoils of war to be thrown out in front of your family."

His hands balled into fists at his sides. She could see how hard he was fighting to hold back the shouting he was dying to do.

"When did you become such a drama queen? This is absurd. No one is treating you like the spoils of war for God's sake. Get a grip."

"So you're saying a marriage is not in the cards?" she asked, hoping he couldn't hear the trembling in her voice.

"Marriage." He sank onto the window seat beside her. A marriage hadn't even been in his calculations. It had taken a lot just to get his family to agree to meet with her. But a marriage?

"I don't think I can do that, Alex," he said, trying to be honest. "Not now. Not yet."

He would do it if he loved you. Again she felt the pain of rejection. Again she knew she'd been asking for it.

"Fine. I won't be presented, then. I won't officially even be here."

She was working hard to make her tone light, to hide the hurt she felt. Better to seem a casual conniver than a victim.

"I'll just be a rumor. I'll stay in the background and skulk around behind the drapes, like a reproachful ghost out of Dickens, making everyone shudder and rethink their dinner plans."

He stared at her and almost laughed, not sure if she were angry or kidding.

"I won't just be a tagalong," she added quite seriously. She had too much pride for that. *Pride goeth before a fall.* She knew that. Too bad. There were some things she just couldn't compromise on.

"Alexandra, try to understand." Reaching out, he took her hands in his and looked earnestly into her eyes. "At this stage, the country is on edge, not sure what is going to work out, what they are going to discard in favor of a new system. I'm going to be crowned king in a few weeks. Once that happens, things may stabilize. I just don't know. I have to think of my people first."

She nodded, suddenly very tired. "I know that," she murmured, feeling lost and hopeless.

"I've made everyone else in the family conform to these rules. I've fought hard to keep our comings and goings and crazy mistakes out of the tabloids. I've even forced my brothers to have low-key weddings in order to avoid riling up the populace." He shook his head, pleading with his eyes that she understand. "How could I fly in their faces and marry an Acredonna? It's inconceivable."

She frowned, wondering. "Do you really feel there is that much hatred against my family in this country?"

He winced, hesitated, and then went on. "In a word, yes. I'm sorry, Alex. Your father was brutal. Your brothers aren't much better."

She closed her eyes. "I know that."

"Don't you see? If I marry you, there are factions in this country who will be afraid the old regime is coming back into power. And then there will be those who warn me to be careful, since this is all a plot concocted by your father in the first place, in order to get a wedge into this administration. When fears run so high, paranoia runs even higher. I can't risk a civil war right now."

She nodded slowly. "All right," she said so softly it was almost a whisper. "We'll have to wait, Robbie and I." Looking up, she wanted to make sure he understood they were a joint item. He didn't get Robbie without her. No one ever would.

He looked deep into her eyes, then, his face softening, he raised her hand to his lips and kissed her fingers. "I'd still like to present you to my family, Alex," he said. "Please think it over." Rising, he left the room.

Alex rose as well, starting to see him to the exit. But he left too quickly and she was alone. Closing her eyes, she leaned against the door and her sigh came from the depths of her soul. This couldn't go on forever, but no matter how hard she tried, she couldn't see an end to it. At least, not a good one.

Was she going to be happy here? She couldn't see how that could happen, not under these circumstances. But she would try to adjust.

Grace came in to take Robbie for his bath. She noted that Grace seemed to be in her element, as comfortable here as she had seemed before. Maybe she was just a more adaptable person.

"Or maybe I'm just a crank," she muttered as she went into her own room to lie down and rest before dinner. Surely that was what Dane thought right now. And maybe he was right.

Dane couldn't get that kiss he'd shared with Alex at the stream out of his mind. It had been a simple kiss. Hardly more than a sweet gesture of affection. But he found himself obsessing over it by the hour, remembering how her hair had blown against his face, how her fresh scent had filled his head, how soft her skin had been, how warm her body.

He stopped, angry at himself. What the hell was he doing? He was about to be crowned king of Carnethia and all he could think about was that woman. He had a country to run, a country to save from the brink of disaster. And yet, there she was, elusive and mysterious, just out of reach, the owner of his heart, the target of his anger.

The more she pulled away, the more he wanted her.

He wasn't young and he wasn't inexperienced, and yet he was acting like a teenager. He'd had lots of women—beautiful women, pleasant women, women that were fun to be with. Women who were instantly forgettable.

Alex wasn't one of them. He would never forget her as long as he lived. She would always be that ache in his heart.

He remembered how close they had been that weekend in Tokyo. They had spent hours tangled together, her head on his chest, his face in her hair. They'd talked and talked and completely convinced themselves that they could perform miracles—that they could talk their families into condoning a relationship between the two of them.

"We'll do it. We'll hold hands and jump across the rift."

He knew now that they'd had no real idea how big and deep that rift could be. But they found out soon enough.

And now she was back in his life, but just out of reach. He could see her, smell her, taste her, but he couldn't really have her. Was he going to end up living a virtual life instead of a real one?

He had to go back to basics. His country needed a queen. How could he marry anyone else while Alex lived just a few steps away? The idea was preposterous. It would have been hard enough to do under any circumstances, but to have her so close, taking care of his son— Marriage to someone else, even an arranged marriage that was all business, would be impossible. Couldn't be done.

There was only one remedy he could think of. It seemed impossible, as well, but the more he thought about it, the more he began to wonder if perhaps…just perhaps…

No, he was crazy to even think such things. He needed to step back, get some perspective. He was letting his fantasies run away with his brain. Maybe he should call in his brothers and get a little feedback. He began to play with the idea. It had promise.

Alex fumed about Dane's plan to present her to his family for the next few days. She stayed in her own room when he came to visit Robbie, only venturing out to say hello just before he left each time. It was painfully clear that they should treat each other as formal partners and nothing closer. Anything else was courting disaster.

He didn't bring up his plan again, but it was always there between them, and she couldn't get over the craziness of it.

What was he thinking? Did he really think he could orchestrate how everyone in his range of influence behaved? Did he think he could make her into the sort of pliable semi-servant such an act would imply? The whole thing made her furious.

And then there was the lack of logic. He was supposedly obsessive about keeping his family affairs out of the papers. Right now she was sure she was the subject of a lot of rumors in the palace, but things had been kept under control. So far, so good. Once her presence here was out in the open, no one was going to feel constrained from calling their favorite reporter and spilling the beans.

"We have to be very careful, we don't want the media getting wind of this."

She heard that from someone she dealt with at least once a day. The whole palace was running scared all the time. She asked Carla why.

"Because everyone is terrified of Dane, of course."

Alex stared. "Terrified of Dane? Whatever for?"

Carla blinked. "He's a very scary guy."

"What would he do to anyone who talked?" she asked, at sea.

"He'd be very, very angry," she said. "You should see some of the lectures our cousin Nadia gets. She attracts a lot of press and he hates it."

Alex could only shake her head and marvel at how much their conditioning had taught them to react like trained seals to everything Dane did and said. But she supposed that was part of what made him a natural for the crown. He already had the fear factor going for him.

Hah! Was she the only one who was immune?

She had her own theory on what should be done about the tabloids.

"Tell them everything," she advised the next time she and Dane talked about it. "Make the place an open book. Don't keep any secrets. They ferret them out every time, anyway. Why not be the one to bring something out? That way you can put your own interpretation on it."

"You're very naive," he growled at her. "You don't know what you're talking about."

"Here's what I think," she said, ignoring his grumpy reaction. "Go straight to the people. Tell them everything. Bypass the press and set up direct communication with your subjects. They'll get the true story and they'll love you for it. Trust them."

He laughed at her and she shrugged.

"Suit yourself," she said. "But you'll see. The more you try to hide things, the worse it is when they finally come out. Think about it."

Though he'd scorned her advice at the time, he did think about it, and when it came right down to brass tacks, he realized her ideas weren't half-bad. In fact, the more he knew about her, the more he respected just about everything about her. The irony was, she would make a perfect queen for him. If only she weren't an Acredonna.

Her very existence was playing havoc with

his peace of mind. Every time he visited Robbie, though he loved the baby more than he'd ever expected to love another human being, half of his heart was yearning for the woman he knew was waiting in the next room.

He couldn't go on this way. He needed help. It was time to call in his brothers and see what he could work out. He didn't have a lot of hope when he set up the meeting with them, but he had to try. He was going crazy.

In the end he added Carla to the mix. It might be good to get a woman's view as well. He called them all in to a working breakfast on the flagstone terrace that jutted out from his bedroom, overlooking the rose gardens.

They arrived, one by one, not sure what they'd been called together for. Watching them come in, he felt a wave of affection for them all. His brother Nico was so serious, and recently so heartbroken, and now so happy with his new love, Marisa, who was about to have a baby. His brother Mychale had found happiness as well with Abby and the little girl baby, Brianna. His sister, Carla, was unattached, but the St. Tupin's Day Ball was supposed to help take care of that. Hopefully one of the young, eligible bachelors invited would take an interest in her and offer for her hand.

His parents were both gone now, and at times like this, he felt their loss deeply. His father's whole mission in life had been to get Carnethia back into royal hands where it belonged. Well, they'd done it, only to find that to achieve their goal only meant the beginning of their problems. Running a country wasn't easy. Not if you wanted to do it right.

He turned his gaze on his siblings as they took their places at the table and then he cleared his throat.

This was unusual. He knew they all often considered him an ogre. Dictatorial. Authoritarian. But after all, he was going to be king in a few weeks. Someone taking that sort of power had to be careful to maintain a sense of command, and he knew he'd done that with gusto at times.

But this would be different. This time *he* needed *them*.

"I want your advice," he said once he had their attention.

"Our advice?" Carla echoed, wide-eyed. "Us? Are you sure?"

"Well, this is a new twist," Prince Mychale said, humor gleaming in his blue eyes. "I don't know if we're ready for this."

Dane's good mood was fast evaporating and he frowned at them all. "Are you finished with the comedy routines?" he asked coldly.

"Let's hear what Dane has to say," Prince Nico suggested, giving the two rebels a quelling look.

"Well, of course," Carla said with a shrug.

"What kind of advice are we talking about?" Mychale asked suspiciously.

Dane hesitated, not sure how he wanted to put this. "In a way, I'm going to ask your permission."

"Hah! Are we allowed to say no?" Mychale said sardonically as he slouched appealingly in his chair.

Dane controlled his temper with effort. "That's why I'm asking you," he said carefully. "You can say yes or no. That doesn't mean I'm necessarily going to do what you say."

"Of course not," Carla chortled.

"But I want you to give me your honest opinion. In fact, that's exactly what I need."

"Then I say no," Mychale said, slapping the flat of his hand down on the table. "That's what you always say to anything I want to do."

"Me, too," Carla chimed in, teasing. "It's always no, no, no to everything I ask about."

Even Nico was chuckling now. "I guess you're going to get a taste of your own medicine," he told Dane with a grin.

Dane worked hard to keep his temper. There were times when he'd been accused of seeming to lack a real sense of humor, especially when the joke was on him. He had to admit, this might just be one of those times. But the situation was just too important to him to mess around with.

"If you're not going to be serious about this, we aren't going to go on," he said, his clenched jaw making it hard to get his words out fluently.

"Sorry." Carla scrunched down in her seat. "I'll be good. Honest."

Mychale didn't say anything but he sat up taller and gave his brother an apologetic look that seemed to fit the bill.

"Okay," Dane said, his jaw jutting out. "You all know about Alexandra."

They nodded.

"You know that she and I…that we… Well, we had Robbie together. You understand that he's my son and will be the new crown prince once I take the throne."

Nods came from each sibling once again, as they stared at their older brother intently. So far nothing he'd said was news.

"And you know that I…care a lot about Alex."

This time no one nodded, but they began to look a bit uneasy.

Dane gazed around at the group and steeled himself for opposition. "So. What do you suppose would happen if I married her?"

A shock wave sizzled through the group, and then the looks of horror began to contort each face.

"Marry an Acredonna?" Mychale said. "Are you crazy? You can't do that."

Dane glared at him. "She's the mother of my child."

Nico shook his head. "Dane, she's the enemy. The people will never accept it."

All three talked at once and he roared them back into order, then let each speak in turn. The consensus was overwhelmingly negative. Every argument he brought up, every simple, fragile hope, got knocked down by every one of them.

After a painful session of opposition, the crown prince's face had grayed. His eyes looked bleak. "You just can't see any way it can be done?" he asked at last.

One by one, each sibling shook his or her head.

"All right, then," their older brother said gruffly. "Think it over though, will you? If you think of any way…"

They filed out slowly, looking as disturbed and sad as he felt. But he knew they were right. It wouldn't work. The country wasn't ready for it. The people would be outraged. This wasn't medieval times when a ruler could just impose his will on his people. Their will had to be taken into consideration.

But he could hardly bear it. How could he go on seeing her every day and not be able to touch her, kiss her, hold her body and feel her respond?

There was only one answer. He was going to have to find some way to avoid seeing her every time he went in to see his son. Just the brief interludes they had together built the agony. The more he saw her, the more he wanted her. With feelings that strong, something was bound to set off an explosion. Until he figured out a way to avoid that, he'd best stay away entirely.

CHAPTER NINE

ALEX sat in the window seat tapping her foot impatiently, turning to look at the clock for the fifth time in the last two minutes. It was time to face facts. He wasn't coming. Again.

It had been over two days since he'd come to see his baby. They had barely been there a week and already he was slacking off in his fatherly duties. If this was how things were going to be, she wouldn't stand for it.

She'd sent him a message that morning letting him know they expected to see him at ten o'clock. It was ten-thirty. He wasn't coming.

"All right, then, Mr. Crown Prince," she muttered, sliding off the seat and ringing for Grace. "If you won't come to the mountain, the mountain will come to you."

A few minutes later she was striding down the hall toward the main house. She hadn't been on that side since the night they'd arrived. But she was going now, powered by anger. She would not allow Dane to ignore his baby.

A tiny suspicion surfaced for just a moment. Could a part of her anger be on her own account? She missed him. She knew she did. She longed to see him, no matter how crazy he made her.

Sure, that was part of it. But why not? He was avoiding her. There were plenty of good reasons why he should be doing exactly that. Fine, but he couldn't take it out on their baby.

She entered the main hall and found a maid polishing silver in a side room near the kitchen.

"Hello," she said to the startled girl. "I'm looking for Crown Prince Dane. Can you tell me where he is?"

Mutely she pointed toward the area of the palace that housed the library and various conference rooms. Alex knew them well.

"Is he in the boardroom?" she asked the girl.

"Yes, miss. I think they're having a meeting or something."

"Right. Thanks." Wheeling, she changed direction, heading for the business side of the building. An elegantly dressed older woman suddenly stepped into her path, coming from the library.

"Excuse me," Alex said, stepping around her with a slight curtsy.

"Oh, dear," cried Lady Julia, reaching out to stop herself from falling. "Oh, dear me!"

An elderly gentleman with a monocle appeared behind her.

"Look!" she said to him. "It's that dreadful Acredonna woman."

Alex didn't let it break her stride for a moment. She kept going, rounding a turn and heading into the study reception area. The nice-looking young woman who sat at a desk near the tall, mahogany double doors glanced up in surprise as Alex came to a stop before her.

"The crown prince," she said shortly. "Where is he?"

"He's…he's in a cabinet meeting right now," the secretary said quickly. "You can't see him. He's busy. If you'd like to wait…"

She wasn't waiting. If she did that, all her

anger would seep away and she would end up wimping out. She wasn't about to let that happen. Instead, she started toward the boardroom.

"But you can't go in there," the secretary cried, trying to bar her way.

"Yes, I can. I've been there before."

She didn't want to be rude and say, "Just try to stop me," in actual words but her smile said it loud and clear, and she sailed right past, pushing open the door and barging straight into the room.

Four men and two women stared at her as she entered, two of them Dane's brothers. And then there was Dane. He stood at the head of the table, a pointer in his hand and a bulletin board behind him, and he didn't look happy about the intrusion.

Too bad. She wasn't exactly in a cheerful mood herself.

"Excuse me, ladies and gentlemen," she said with aplomb, nodding to one side of the long table, then the other. "I'm sorry to interrupt your meeting. I'm sure it's very important and very interesting."

She turned to Dane. "Your Highness?" she

said politely. "I'd like a private word with you, please."

Annoyance flashed in his blue eyes. He stood like a man who wasn't going anywhere and waved a hand toward the others. "I'm in the middle of a cabinet meeting, Alex," he said with cold precision. "I'm a little busy."

"So I see." She scanned the others, expecting to see annoyance. To her surprise, they seemed watchful and almost amused. "What's the topic?" she asked brightly.

Dane glared at her. "Trade," he snapped, looking toward the doorway where the secretary was waving apologetically to him. "You wouldn't be interested."

"A serious issue," she allowed cheerfully. "I'm sure it's very important."

"It is," Dane said shortly, trying to stare her down. "We're working on finding opportunities for trade with Tahiti." He jerked his head toward the door, indicating the route he wished she would take. "Now if you'll just…"

"Ah, Tahiti," she said, tilting her head as though listening to tropic breezes flowing past. "Warm sunshine, turquoise water. But I didn't know we were delving into the coconut trade."

A strangled choking sound from one side of the table told her she'd hit a nerve.

"We may start," Prince Mychale said with a deadpan expression that belied the sparkle of humor in his eyes. "That way we'll have an excuse to go there on holiday. Get it?"

"Oh, I get it." She smiled at him hopefully and was gratified to have him grin right back. It could have gone the other way. She really had no idea how anyone in the royal family felt about her other than Carla, and she'd had some disappointing evidence from Lady Julia in the hallway.

But Mychale seemed receptive enough. She liked the casual insouciance of his manner. And he was awfully nice to look at. Almost as nice as his big brother.

"Alex, why are you here?" Dane challenged. "Do you actually have an opinion on this matter? Something we should know?"

"Heavens no," she said, waving it away. "I'm no expert on trade." She turned to look him straight in the eye, hands on her hips. "I am, however, an expert on babies at the moment." She looked at the members and noticed they were pretty much all grinning by now. "And I'm here because I invited you to a meeting with a certain baby and you didn't show up. So I came along to lobby for 'babies'." She turned to pin Dane to the wall again with her stare. "I need the topic of 'babies' to move up on your list of priorities."

His brows came together ominously. "I'll think about it," he said with a dismissive gesture. "Just go, Alex," he added in a low whisper out of the side of his mouth that only she was supposed to hear.

"No." She shook her head, looking at him with fierce intensity. "You don't have to think about anything. You just have to do it."

He stared at her, at a loss to understand why she was doing this to him. "I'll drop by and see you later about this," he said.

"No." She was pleasant but insistent. "Now. I want you to come with me right now."

She glared at him and he started to glare back, but both his brothers began snickering and he had to glare at them instead.

"Please," she said earnestly. "I mean it, Your Highness. You need to come with me now."

He looked at her, then looked at Nico and Mychale. For some reason, he didn't seem to have any options left. He knew why she was here, knew what she wanted, and felt guilty as hell about it. He'd been ignoring his baby and all because he was trying to avoid seeing Alex. It had been a dumb move. He needed to make up for it. Oh well, there was no use prolonging the agony.

"All right." Throwing down the pointer, he flashed a look back at his cabinet. "I'll be back in ten minutes."

"He'll be back after lunch," she corrected sweetly. "You all might as well take a lunch break. So long!"

The silence that enveloped them as they walked out of the room erupted into laughter they could hear as they made their way to the main hallway.

"Alex," he began. "I can't believe you would interrupt a cabinet meeting for this."

"Believe it," she said coolly. "And believe that I will do it again if I have to. You're not going to ignore Robbie."

He started to say something but she cut him off. "I don't care why you did it. You may have a whole set of wonderful, compelling reasons. But they won't fly. Because Robbie comes first. Remember that."

To her surprise he muttered something she couldn't hear, but he didn't fight back. He came along willingly enough and spent an hour playing with the baby. He even had his lunch sent in on a tray along with hers.

They sat side by side, eating off small tables brought in for their convenience. At first neither one of them spoke, and she wondered what he was thinking. Did he resent what she'd done? She couldn't tell for sure.

"He almost started to crawl this morning," she said at last.

Dane turned to look at her. "He did? What happened?"

She smiled. She was definitely relieved that he was still emotionally engaged with Robbie. Now that he'd come back she could admit to herself how scared she'd been that he might have begun to lose interest. But all evidence pointed the other way at the moment.

"I put him down on his back near the sunlight, turned away for a minute, and when I turned back, he was on his stomach and starting to push up. He was feeling out what his legs could do."

Dane's smile was pure, candid joy. "No kidding."

"He'll be crawling any minute now. Guaranteed."

He nodded toward where her cell phone lay on the desk. "You call me when he does it, okay? I want to be here for his first real crawl."

She laughed. "It's usually the first step that dads are interested in," she said.

"That's too far away. I've got to see the crawl."

"You got it."

They smiled into each other's eyes. Then Dane turned away, groaning.

"Alex, this is exactly why I was trying to stay away," he told her.

She nodded, her eyes suddenly stinging. "Oh, yes, I understand," she said, blinking rapidly. She'd known it all along. The two of them together were like kindling left near a roaring fire.

She turned toward him, her eyes huge with tragedy. "I'll leave before you come," she said gravely. "Just give me set times and I can make sure we don't see each other at all."

He looked deep into her eyes and shook his head slowly. "No," he said. "That won't work."

She shrugged. "Then what will?"

"I don't know."

She nodded slowly. She had to agree with that. "But you can't let Robbie suffer for it."

"No. That wasn't any good. We'll just have to take it as it comes. See what happens."

That might be all they had for the moment, but it sounded dangerous. They were going to have to think of something better.

"By the way," he said, just before he left her. "I've contacted Henri and told him you would like him to join you here."

"Oh, Dane!" She jumped up, clapping her hands together. "Thank you. You don't know how much I appreciate that."

He nodded. "I'm hoping to make you as comfortable as possible. I think you're right. I think you must establish your own identity here. I don't want you to be treated like a servant by anyone."

"Good." He understood. She was so gratified by that, she almost cried. "Thank you."

"Alex." He stood in front of her, shaking his head, wanting to say something, but somehow the words wouldn't come. "Oh, hell," he swore harshly, turning and striding from the room.

Her phone rang a half hour later. It was Marque, the younger of her two brothers. She liked him better than she liked Ivan, but he was pretty goofy most of the time. She picked it up, flipped it open and put it to her ear.

"Hello?"

"So, there you are." He said it as though he could see her.

"Here I am," she admitted.

"I heard the Montenevadas got you. Is that true?"

"It is."

"Uh-huh. The bastards."

She sighed. "Speak for yourself, Marque."

"Are they treating you well?"

She shrugged. "About as well as can be expected."

"Good. Don't do anything to screw it up."

She frowned and wrinkled her nose. "What are you talking about?"

"We're going to need your eyes and ears inside the palace. You're our own little private mole."

Oh, the horror. "Marque, what are you planning?"

"You'll know in due time. All will be clear. Just be ready to help out when the time comes."

"Okay."

She waited but he didn't say anything more. "So that's it?" she asked.

"Pretty much," he admitted.

She shook her head. "You don't want to know if I'm being questioned? Tortured?"

"Are you?" That piqued his interest.

"I go on the rack and get stretched every night, but you don't care."

"They put in a rack? Cool!"

She rolled her eyes. "Goodbye, Marque."

"No, wait! Tell me about the rack."

She clicked off. From what she'd heard her brothers were busy as little bees organizing the exile community right now. There was even a large group of exiles who had collected together in Brazil and they were very supportive of her brothers' nutty schemes. She just hoped they kept themselves occupied with all this planning. That way, an actual execution of their plot wouldn't get underway for years.

Still, it made her realize that Dane was taking on a lot of risk by letting her stay here. For all he knew, she was a hundred percent behind her brothers and their craziness. No wonder he was having her watched.

The reunion with Henri was quite emotional. He came into the room and she jumped up from the window seat to throw herself at him.

"Oh Henri, thank you so much for coming."

She threw her arms around his neck and gave him a big kiss on his weathered cheek. "You don't know how I've missed you."

"I would do anything for you, Miss," he said, looking at her with love, like a benign grandfather. "You know that. Anything to make sure you have what you need."

"You are such a dear. I've been lost without you." She sighed happily. "Did they give you a room? Where is it?"

They chatted for a few more minutes, catching up. And then Henri gave her some bad news.

"Your father is growing weaker by the day. And, miss, when I was there, he asked for you."

"He did?" She gazed at him, startled by the thought. "I'd better make plans to go to him, then." Her mouth was dry and she realized the thought terrified her. What if she went and couldn't come back? But she had to go. And she knew she would have to leave her baby behind when she did. Another dilemma.

"We'll talk about how we're going to do this later," she told Henri. "In the meantime, welcome back to the palace."

"Yes," he said as he turned to go. "I'm glad to be home."

Her smile froze on her face as she watched him disappear out the door. Home. Of course. This place was as much home to him as it was to her—and that meant under previous ownership. But to have him say it so casually shocked her. Despite everything, he was right. This was home.

It was the night of the St. Tupin's Day Ball. Alex could hear the arrivals even from this side of the palace. When she went into the hallway, she could hear the orchestra tuning up. The excitement was contagious.

Grace and a couple of the other servants helped her with the dress Carla had found for her. The fabric was a pale-green silk embroidered with tiny seed pearls. The skirt was full but the neckline swooped down low, showing lots of cleavage and leaving her shoulders bare. She pulled on long gloves and slipped her feet into soft dancing shoes.

"You're so gorgeous," Grace gushed. "Every man in the ballroom will fall instantly in love with you."

"That's not what I'm going for," she answered sensibly. "I just want to spend a little time soaking up the atmosphere. It's been so long—since before the war started—since I've been to a ball like this. It's just for fun."

Her thick, lustrous hair curled languorously around her shoulders, and she pushed it back in order to put her mask in place. Then she picked up the fan that was part of her costume and was off to meet Carla at the south entrance, a place they had agreed on.

Of course Carla wasn't there. Alex stood in the doorway, not sure what to do. People were entering from the main stairway and being introduced on the sound system. She wanted to avoid that at all costs.

The dance floor was filled with dancers, all dressed to kill, and the orchestra was playing a lush waltz arrangement that made her want to sway on her own. She decided to slip in and stay along the wall, the better to observe and not be observed. She found a niche alongside a large column and stayed there, half hidden, watching the dancers.

Prince Mychale was announced, and there he was, looking less like a playboy these days and more like a devoted husband as he escorted his pretty wife, Abby, onto the dance floor. Then she saw Prince Nico helping his wife, Marisa, into a chair across the room. Marisa was astoundingly pregnant yet managed to look beautiful all the same. The woman they called Cousin Nadia swept into view. She was dressed like a high-fashion model and had at least five men following her like happy puppies. Alex laughed softly as she watched them vie for her attention.

Suddenly she caught sight of Dane. He

was dancing with a tall, golden-haired beauty and appearing remarkably bored with it all. Alex hid her smile behind her fan, and at the same moment a handsome, muscular man approached her.

"Hello," he said. "And who is this?"

"Oh." She was startled. She'd hoped to be ignored. "Nobody," she said quickly. "Really. I'm nobody. You wouldn't want to know me, anyway. Take my word for it."

She couldn't have said anything more guaranteed to arouse male interest. In moments he'd persuaded her to join him in just one little dance, which she regretted immediately. Because one dance with him turned into ten with nine other men, and before long, she had one of the longest lines of suitors waiting for turns of any young woman in the room. She knew this was crazy, but she was having a marvelous time. She couldn't have identified any of the men. They were a blur. But they could dance, and that was all she needed to feel she'd found a bit of heaven, for the moment.

And suddenly she was being swept away by the man she'd most hoped to avoid. She saw a wealth of rich auburn hair and the flash of clear-blue eyes behind his black mask, noticed a blindingly white uniform, lots of medals and gold epaulettes, and realized, with a sense of thrill, that it was Dane who held her close and led her out onto the dance floor. Soon she was whirling to his lead.

"What are you doing here?" he muttered close to her ear as he pulled her in close for a dip.

"This isn't me," she tried, feeling giddy. After all, it had worked with the anonymous men she'd been dancing with. "I'm someone else."

"Like hell you are," he growled. "I know Alexandra when I have her in my arms."

She laughed. "Oh, Dane, don't burst this bubble. Let it float for a few more minutes. I'm having such a lovely time."

"Carla put you up to this, didn't she?" he said, his gaze sweeping over the lovely expanse of naked skin she was presenting to the world. "Carla is behind every little plot I uncover in this place."

His voice displayed more humor than anger, and she didn't feel she had to jump to Carla's defense.

"I'm not going to tattle on your sister, but you're not far wrong. She's an adorable imp, isn't she?"

"Some might call it that," he said dryly. "Others might say the word *meddling* comes to mind."

They danced. And danced some more. He wouldn't let anyone else have her. He held her as though she were an angel that he was about to reluctantly set free to fly in the clouds. She clung to him as though she were in love. And maybe she was.

The music, the lights, the people swirling past, the incredibly wide shoulders right there for her to lean on, and the arms of a future king holding her close—it was all completely intoxicating and wonderful.

But finally she knew she had to go.

"It's late," she said, gazing at his strong chin and wondering why she'd never noticed before how chiseled it looked. Movie-star quality. No doubt about it. Maybe it was the mask that set it off and made it so obvious. Whatever. She was in love with a chin.

"I've stayed much longer than I planned to. I have to get back."

"Why?" he asked, and suddenly he was nuzzling near her ear. "Is your carriage going to turn into a pumpkin, Cinderella?"

She laughed, enjoying the exquisite shivers his touch set up on her skin. "If I leave a glass slipper behind, will you search for me?"

He drew back so that he could look into her face, or at least as much of it as he could see, and he smiled. "What do I get once I find you?"

"If it were up to me…" She let her voice trail off and he knew exactly what she was implying. She touched his cheek. It was a gesture of endearment.

"Are you angry that I crashed the party?" she asked him.

"No." He dropped a soft kiss on her lips and added, "The party didn't begin until I had you in my arms."

She sighed, letting the warmth of his obvious desire sweep over her. "Ditto," she whispered.

He led her out through the open French doors, into the artificial forest at the edge of the terrace.

"Dane," she said, looking around and realizing he'd brought her out beyond the edge of the lights from the ballroom, out into the shadows where no one else had ventured. "Why are we out here?"

He smiled down at her, cradling her body with his own. "So I can kiss you properly," he said, his voice husky with urgency. "I didn't burst your bubble, Alex. Don't burst mine."

She had no intention of doing anything of the sort. With a sigh of sweet surrender, she lifted her arms around his neck and raised her face to his. His mouth found hers and she opened to his tongue, meeting it with her own special greed. He tasted of maleness and appetite and a hint of wine. She'd never known anything to be quite so sweet and so dangerously provocative at the same time.

He pulled her close and began to drop soft, hot kisses on her skin, starting at her collarbone and traveling down onto the swell of her breasts. She moaned softly, beginning to melt.

"You're addictive, Alex," he murmured, still devouring her skin with his lips. "I want to taste every inch of you."

She arched back to let him plunge into her neckline, loving the way her breasts felt to his touch. And then he pulled her up against his hard, muscular body and she gasped as she felt his hunger press against her.

She wanted him, needed him, had to have his love as she'd had it that weekend in Tokyo. All logic, all thinking was gone and she only existed to be his other half. Surely he could sense it, surely he would find a way for them to—

"Dane! Dane! Come quick. Marisa is having her baby!"

He pulled back, breathing hard and swearing softly.

"Oh," she moaned faintly, blinking rapidly as she came up for air.

"Marisa's having her baby," he explained to her, still groggy himself with the fog of arousal.

"Yes, I heard," she said, laughing softly at him. "You'd better go."

He still held her. "I don't want to lose you," he said, sinking his face in her thick hair.

All humor drained from her face. "Oh, Dane, I don't want to lose you, either."

He drew back. They stared into each other's eyes for a long moment, and finally he pulled away, still looking reluctant to leave.

"Go," she said. "I'll see you in the morning."

He nodded, cupped her cheek with his hand, and then he was gone.

Alex stared after him, still floating on a cloud of happiness. This was what it felt like to be in love with a wonderful man. By morning she would have to hide it again, but for now, she was going to wallow in it for all she was worth.

CHAPTER TEN

"It isn't that I resent Marisa having her baby in the middle of my coming out," Carla explained, though no one had accused her of anything of the sort. "It's just that once again, other, bigger events seem to come in to overshadow the little princess's search for a suitable husband. First it's the war, then it's the rebuilding, finally it's my own darn sister-in-law showing off her baby birthing expertise. One does begin to wonder if this marrying stuff is just not in the cards for me."

"You'll find someone. Or he will find you. Never fear." Alex sighed. "By the way, where were you? I couldn't find you when I went to the ballroom. We were supposed to meet at the south entry."

"Oh." Carla looked chagrined. "Sorry about

that. I saw someone I hadn't seen for a while and we…sort of got to talking, and— Well, I forgot. I'm really sorry that happened. I should have paid more attention to the clock."

"No problem. I had a good time, anyway."

"So I heard." Carla gave her a significant look. "They say the men were stacked like cordwood all around you all evening."

Grace came in the room with Robbie, freshly clean from his bath, before Alex could respond, and Carla jumped up to take him in her arms. She gave Grace a quick grin and Alex smiled, thinking Carla was just about the friendliest princess she knew. Then her smile dimmed as she watched Grace and Carla exchange a few quips. If she didn't know better, she would think they just might be old friends.

But that was crazy. How could they have known each other in the past? She'd hired Grace in Paris under a recommendation of the doctor, Gregor Narna.

Still, something about their coziness bothered her. Having grown up in Altamere herself, she knew more than she wanted to remember about palace plots. As a result, she hated deceit and the impression of having things going on behind her back. She prized honesty and straight-forward openness above all else. She didn't mind so much if people disagreed with her or even worked against her, as long as they did so above the board and didn't play games.

She told herself she must be imagining things. She adored both Carla and Grace. Why should she suspect them of plotting? There was no reason for it. And she put it out of her mind.

By the end of the week, Alex had decided to let Dane present her at dinner and now she was as nervous as she'd ever been.

"Oh, phooey, they're not going to bite," Carla told her when she confided in the princess.

"I'm not so sure. You should have seen Lady Julia gaping at me in the hall the other day," she told her.

Carla waved that away. "Pay her no mind. She's skittish, but lovable in the end. You'll see."

Carla helped her pick out a long yellow silk pantsuit to wear for the event.

"Understated yet elegant," she said, nodding her approval when Alex tried it on. "They'll all love you in no time. Don't worry. They're just people."

Just people, but very special people with a very serious ability to affect her life and the life of her child. That was why she'd decided she had to do it. She needed to build a position for herself. Without standing, she wouldn't have a way to protect Robbie against whatever storms would buffet him in the future. She had to make a place for herself so that she could make a secure place for him.

"I'm compromising my principles to do this," she reminded Dane later that day when she told him her decision.

"I know," he said with a distracted smile, "and believe me, I appreciate it."

But his mind was on other things.

"There's a problem with Carla," he finally told her after she probed to find out what was bothering him.

She threw up her hands. "Well, of course there's a problem with Carla. Carla was born to make trouble. She can't help it."

"You hit the nail on the head there," he said ruefully.

"So what exactly is it this time?"

"I'll tell you. It's frustrating. Here, all these years, she's been complaining that no one is taking her need for a husband seriously. Now there are at least three eminently eligible bachelors from the ball last night who've signaled interest in being given permission to begin courting her." He shook his head. "She's rejected every one of them."

"What?" Alex was surprised to hear it. "I thought she was so eager to have a little romance in her life."

He nodded. "That's what I thought, too. But she's waved them all off."

Alex frowned, remembering some of the things Carla had said lately. She'd been prone to cryptic comments when it came to the ball. In fact, now that she thought of it, Carla had hinted there might be someone else she was interested in.

"Suppose she had someone else in the wings," she said speculatively to Dane. "Someone not quite so eligible. What then?"

"Then she'd better get rid of him," Dane said curtly.

Alex's eyes widened. "What do you mean? Your brothers both married women who would probably be considered…well, not quite suitable. I think."

"Yes. Exactly." He jabbed the air with his forefinger. "And that trend has got to be nipped in the bud."

"I see." She saw only too well. Trouble was coming. She could sense it brewing on the horizon. She only hoped it would stop at the edge of the palace grounds.

She went to visit Marisa and the new baby. No one balked when she asked if she would be allowed. So she went and no one turned a hair. Marisa lay back against the pillows looking proud and tired, and Alex remembered feeling very much the same way. Only, Marisa had her husband, Nico, sitting at the edge of the bed, looking just as tired and just as proud. That was the way it ought to be.

"You have a beautiful baby," she told the new parents.

They nodded their agreement and thanked her, and she went back to her room feeling happy and at the same time, rather sad.

"Melancholy, they call it," she explained to Grace when she asked what the matter was. She was in a melancholy mood.

She walked along the hallways, getting a little exercise, and as she looked out the tall windows at the ground below, she noticed a beautifully dressed woman with a retinue taking a turn in the rose garden. Something about that woman chilled her. She went back to her room and got Grace to come take a look.

"Who is that out in the rose garden?"

Grace came up beside her and peered. "Oh, didn't you see her last night at the ball?"

"No. I was a little busy."

"I heard." Grace nodded, looking wise, and Alex made a face at her.

"So who is she?"

"She's some sort of Italian countess or something. She's staying for the weekend. The word is, she's being touted as the perfect queen for the crown prince."

"What?"

Grace avoided her gaze. She knew the score, but she shook her head and decided she might as well lay it on the line for Alex. "He needs to marry, you know. There are supposedly negotiations going on right now."

Alex's heart began to thump heavily in her chest. "She's very beautiful," she said, and suddenly felt out of breath.

"And they say she's very charming, as well," Grace added, twisting the knife.

"I'm sure she is," Alex said faintly as Grace returned to her duties.

Alex's heart plummeted. She had a painful vision of a future living in the same palace where Dane and his gorgeous bride resided. What would she be then? Still the mother of the crown prince, but not much else. And most of all, Dane's love would be forever denied to her.

There it was, the guilty secret. She still hoped that somehow they would bc able to do what they'd promised each other years ago, to join hands and leap across that rift. She loved him and she yearned with all her heart to have his love in return.

Yes, she was a fool all right. A fool for love.

* * *

"I hear your future bride is staying here," she said to Dane the next morning when he came to visit Robbie.

He gave her a skeptical look. "What are you talking about?"

"The Italian countess?"

"Oh." It was obvious he knew who that was. He'd needed a bit of reminding, but still, he knew. "Yes, well… Never mind that."

Never mind that. As if she could get it out of her mind. Ever since she'd seen the woman, she'd been haunted by a dull, sinking sensation in the pit of her stomach.

Think things are going a bit wrong, babe? her mind was taunting her. *You ain't seen nothin' yet.*

And it turned out her mind was right, because there was more bad news to come. The tabloids had finally noticed her presence at the palace and they were going to play with that fact like a cat with a wounded mouse.

Later in the afternoon, Grace brought the city newspaper in and showed it to her.

"What's this?" she asked.

"Just take a look," Grace advised. "You'd better be prepared for questions."

She spread the paper out and looked at the front page. The headlines were trumpeting the usual tragic events all over the world. But there was also a headline pertaining to Alex and her situation here at the palace.

Rebel Beauty Being Held in Castle, said one headline. Rapunzel, Rapunzel, Let Down Your Hair, screamed another.

"They've finally got the story," Grace noted dryly. "Heaven help us all."

Alex was trembling. She read the article attached to the headlines and groaned aloud, her head in her hands.

"How is Dane taking this?" she asked once she could speak without screaming.

"He's ranting and pacing like a caged tiger," Grace said. "He won't get over this one anytime soon."

Alex nodded. "I know he hates this," she murmured. If only she could think of a way to make him feel better about it. But there wasn't a way. Still, she could give him advice on how to take it.

"There's only one way to fight this sort of

thing," she told him, once she found where he was hiding out.

"Really," he said, skepticism dripping from his tone. "You have the secret."

"Yes, actually. You confront it head-on. Make your life an open book. Ignore the papers and go directly to the people."

He grimaced like a man in pain. "Tell them everything," he said as though it were a cockamamie idea. "In other words, go to the people and tell them why I've got you locked up here in the castle?"

She winced. "You might want to reword that a little."

He thought about that for a moment, then eyed her with growing interest. "It wouldn't bother you to have them know it all?"

"No," she said stoutly. "They're going to know anyway, eventually. Might as well get it out there in a way that gains you credit instead of making you look sneaky."

He shook his head. "I don't know."

"You are theirs, you know," she said softly. "They own you. They deserve to know what your intentions might be."

He thought that one over, then smiled sardonically. "Your family didn't do that. They never opened up to the people, did they?"

"I know," she said earnestly. "And look what happened to us."

He stared into her innocent eyes. It just might be that she had something there. He wasn't going to rule it out without a second thought. Lord, but he was glad she was here. How had he ever lived without her?

He glanced at his watch. "I'm going to have to cut this short, Alex," he said distractedly. "I've got to go show the Italian countess the stables. She's thinking of riding out to the Loralee Hills in the morning, and I promised I'd help her pick out a suitable mount."

"Oh." Alex's heart did a swan dive into her shoes. "Of course. Will I see you later?"

He hesitated. "I doubt it. We're having a sort of mini state dinner tonight. Hopefully I'll be able to come by in the morning."

"After your ride to the Loralee Hills."

"Uh, perhaps. I should be back by noon."

"By noon." She tried to smile but her smile wasn't working so well. "Fine. Have a nice evening."

He hardly seemed to notice as she left the

room. Evidently, his mind was already on the Italian countess and her riding problems. Alex walked briskly back to her side of the palace, trying to let exercise blot out misery. But it didn't really work.

As she passed the French doors that opened onto the vine-covered side terrace, she noticed a movement that made her step back and look again. It was Gregor Narna, Robbie's doctor. She recognized him immediately. With that black patch over one eye, he was hard to miss. He was standing just beyond a twining cypress. What in the world was he doing here? She went to the door, intending to call to him and ask if his presence had anything to do with her son, when she realized he had someone in his arms and was kissing her with passionate intensity. Her hand went to her mouth as she realized who that someone was.

Carla. Dane's sister and Dr. Narna were locked in a torrid embrace that looked as if they both meant business. Alex backed away and turned to head for her room, her mind churning.

Carla and Dr. Narna? Wait a minute. That meant that…

No. She didn't like what this meant. She didn't like it at all. She'd noticed hints of something going on for days, and now she knew she should have been more curious to get to the bottom of it. Somehow Carla and the doctor and Grace were all tied together and had been for a long time. And exactly where did that leave Alex?

"Holding the bag," she muttered, anger growing inside her.

She debated confronting Grace to find out what she knew, but decided to wait until Carla came to visit. It wasn't long before she arrived at the nursery door.

Alex invited her in and asked her to sit down.

"This sounds very serious," Carla said, going quickly from smiling to looking a bit anxious. "What have I done? I hope I haven't said anything that hurt your feelings or makes you angry."

When she didn't get an answering smile from Alex, her own smile completely faded. "Tell me, Alex. What is it?"

Alex closed her eyes to steady herself, then opened them again and began.

"Carla, tell me the truth. What is going on between you and Dr. Narna?"

"Oh." Carla bit her lip. "You saw us?"

She nodded.

Carla sighed. "Well, you might as well know. Everyone else will soon enough. Gregor and I are going to elope." Her eyes widened at her own audacity. "There. I've said it. Don't try to stop us."

Alex's heart felt cold as ice. "But, Carla, how do you know him? What do you know about his background? His family?"

"I've known him forever, Alex," she said earnestly. "He grew up very near our summer home in the lake country. His father was our veterinarian. He sort of—" she blushed prettily "—worshiped me from afar. At least, that's what he claims. A few weeks ago he helped Nico get over a particular syndrome the Montenevada males are susceptible to. And we saw each other again." She shrugged. "It's been all stolen kisses and promises in the dark ever since."

Alex would have smiled if she weren't still suspicious that the relationship was into more than romance. "And Grace?" she asked. "You knew her before, too, didn't you?"

Carla looked startled. "Who told you that?" she said.

"I can see it with my own eyes." Now she was beyond despair and she felt anger rising. "Carla, tell me the truth. Did you send Dr. Narna to me?"

"No! Believe me, Alex, your contacting him was out of the blue. It was only after—"

"Did you have anything to do with me hiring Grace? Did you plan this from the beginning to throw me together with your brother?"

Carla looked suddenly wary. "Maybe."

"Carla!" She couldn't believe she could have been so blind to it. "What right have you to meddle in our affairs?"

Carla's lower lip came out, giving her a stubborn look. "Well, it had been months since Robbie was born and the two of you hadn't done one thing to take care of that problem."

"How did you even know it was a problem? Who told you about my baby? About Dane being the father?"

She looked guilty. "I saw the intelligence reports Dane was getting and I made a few inquiries of my own. I know people who used to work for you, Alex. There are still some left right here in the palace. The rumors were everywhere."

"Rumors!"

"Sometimes a little smoke does mean a great big fire. Once you hired Gregor as your doctor and he reminded me of what a nice person you were, I knew I had to do something. He was just as frustrated about your inability to be proper parents to Robbie as I was. So we were talking about it and it seemed like a good idea to do something to wake the two of you up...."

"Was Dane in on this, too?" she demanded, fury sizzling like a flash flame through her system. She could hardly think, she was so angry.

"Dane? No. Oh no, Alex, he didn't know a thing about it."

So she said. But why should Alex believe her? She would say anything. That much was clear.

"So it was all just a big conspiracy."

"No! Not a conspiracy. A hope. A belief. An opportunity."

Alex didn't buy it. She hated this, hated being manipulated, hated having people pull strings behind her back, making her do things she would never have done if they hadn't interfered. How could she ever trust these people again?

And Dane! He had to have known. She was the only one who didn't have a clue.

That was it, the last straw. She was taking her baby and running. This time she wouldn't get caught. This time, she would leave the country and then she would leave the very continent. She knew of a flight to Brazil that could accommodate her and her baby. She would go live with the exiles. He couldn't get her back from there. And Henri. Thank God he'd let her have Henri. He would take care of things. She was out of here.

Dane returned early from riding with the Italian countess. She was a beautiful woman, perfectly nice, but he couldn't really listen to her when his head was full of Alex. There was only one woman he wanted to be with— be with for all time. His dilemma was finding a way to do that. They couldn't go on this way. Something had to give.

Carla was waiting for him outside his bedroom.

"You've got big trouble," she announced dramatically as he came toward her. "It's Alex. She's really upset."

"What's happened?"

"She knows I had a hand in finding a way for the two of you to meet up again. I'm not sure how much you know."

Following him into his room as he peeled off his shirt and put on a fresh one, preparing to be presentable at lunch, she chattered on, telling him all about Gregor making his services available to an Acredonna, how the two of them had decided Robbie needed his father in his life, how Gregor had recommended Carla's friend Grace as a nanny, how they had made sure the Carnethian intelligence services knew when Alex arrived in Darnam to celebrate her birthday at Chic's.

He grunted. "I'd already figured most of that out," he told her. "Can you hand me my suit coat? Right there on the chair."

She did as he asked. "So you already

knew? You genius. But that's why you've got the top job around here, huh?"

"That and birth order are everything to me," he quipped sardonically.

"Right." She rolled her eyes, then looked at him expectantly. "So what are you going to do about it?"

"About what?"

"About Alex. She's very upset."

He shrugged. "How can I fix that?"

"You've got to marry her, of course."

He stared at her, thunderstruck. "Carla, you were one of the ones telling me, just days ago, that marrying Alex was impossible. Couldn't be done. The world would come to an end if I even tried."

"Sure, it was impossible under normal circumstances, but this is special." She patted his shoulder. "I think, if you approach it the right way, you can do it."

He threw her a baleful look. "Your faith in my powers of persuasion is gratifying," he muttered. "But truth be known, I've been thinking over a few unusual options myself."

"Have you?" She brightened. "Goodie. Now, about me marrying Gregor…"

"One thing at a time, Carla." He managed to look aghast and annoyed in the same expression. "One thing at a time."

CHAPTER ELEVEN

A BIT of time and a lot of thinking brought a measure of sanity to Alex. She was still desperate to escape but she knew she would never get Robbie out of the palace. She would probably find out just how rough Dane could be if she tried it. She knew she was being watched constantly. There was no hope, even if she did get Henri to help her.

But she had to go. She had to get out of here. She was being smothered by her feelings for Dane, her terror for the welfare of her son, her jealousy of the Italian, her resentment at what Carla and Gregor and Grace had done, her prospects for a decent life. Nothing was right, everything was going wrong. She had to get herself some breathing room.

She needed to go see her father, anyway. If

she didn't go soon, he would pass away without her having a chance to ask him to forgive her and say goodbye. But she was still nursing her baby. She couldn't leave him behind and she couldn't take him along. She was caught in a nightmare. What could she do?

Grace came into the room and she stiffened, but the younger woman came straight to where she sat.

"Miss, I know you've talked to Carla," she said candidly. "I know you're very upset and that you think we were conspiring against you." Reaching out, she took Alex's hands in her own. "But that's not true. It wasn't like that at all."

She drew in a deep breath.

"Then tell me, Grace, what was it like?"

She wanted to believe her. Not only did she not like the picture of herself as hapless victim, she liked the nanny a lot—and Robbie responded well to her. It would be awful to have to let her go.

"It's true that Carla and I have been friends for years. We were in school together. I love children and went on to study child care. She went home to be a princess.

When she called me and said Gregor was going to recommend me to you as a nanny, I was thrilled."

Tears stood in Grace's eyes. Alex had to say she was making a very believable case for herself.

"When I met you I loved you right away. And I think you know how I feel about Robbie. I never meant to do anything behind your back."

Alex shook her head. "Then why?"

"I'll tell you how it was. I did know that there were people who were interested in making sure Robbie's father knew about him and had a chance to find him—not to steal him away from you but to help you and the crown prince get back together. That seemed to be a good thing. I'll admit I didn't understand all the aspects that could go wrong. And believe me, I regret not telling you everything I knew as soon as I knew it. I should have done that." She shook her head, blinking back the tears. "When it happened, I was ready to help, but I never planned anything. Carla and I never conspired against you. I hope you can believe me."

Alex squeezed her hands hard and smiled at her. She was beginning to calm down. She still didn't like to think of others trying to manipulate her life, but she realized now they were doing it for what they thought was her own good.

This was a lesson. Don't think you have the answer for others, no matter how benign your intentions.

"I'm glad you've told me this, Grace."

"If you feel you can't trust me anymore, I'll give you my resignation and recommend an agency where you can find a lot of good nannies. But I'm hoping you can forgive me and that we can go on."

Alex drew in a deep, cleansing breath. "Grace, thank you. I'm so happy to be able to trust you again." Reaching out, she gave the girl a hug. "Please stay with us."

Dane came into the nursery and found Alex leaning over the baby's crib. As she looked up, he could see she'd been crying. His heart twisted.

"What's the matter?" he said.

"Nothing," she said.

"Don't lie. No stories, Alex. We've got to have truth between us, remember?"

She turned away, avoiding his gaze. "Please."

"Carla told me that you found out just how conniving she can be."

She nodded. "You weren't a part of it?" she asked, turning back to look at him but just a tiny bit afraid of the answer.

"Of course not."

She smiled. She believed him and that made her feel so much better about it all.

"But I did figure the basics out pretty soon after we got here with you and Robbie. And I can't say I was sorry to have you two with us. But I could tell something was going on."

She shook her head. "You're quicker than I am."

"I had a few more facts than you were aware of." He pulled her close. "Alex, I want us to be honest with each other at all times. Promise?"

She nodded, looking up at him. "I promise."

He kissed her tenderly, then drew back and studied her pretty face as though just seeing it made him happy. "Anyway, I want you to pack up the baby and get ready to travel."

That surprised her. She stepped back and stared at him. "What for? What's going on?"

He looked reluctant, but serious. "You need to go see your father."

Her eyes widened. "Yes, but—"

"But you can't go without Robbie."

"Exactly."

"And he can't go without me."

She stared at him, thunderstruck, not sure she understood. "You're coming with me?" she asked, afraid to believe it.

He sighed, then reached out and grabbed her, pulling her close and dropping a kiss on her startled lips.

"I don't know how I'm going to get through to you with the truth," he told her. "I care about you, Alex. More than you could possibly know."

"Oh, Dane." If she wasn't careful she was going to cry and that would be silly, because she was so happy she was about to burst. Could it really be that Dane, in one mad gesture, had swept away most of her misery? She didn't dare believe it.

"We'll go first thing in the morning," he was saying. "Tonight I have to prepare a broadcast for the nation."

That sounded weighty. "What's the subject? Is there an emergency?"

He smiled and dropped another kiss on her mouth. "You'll know soon enough. Get to bed early and get some sleep. We'll take Grace and Kavon with us. And Henri. I know you can't move a step without Henri."

He was right and she was glad he knew it without having to be told. He was so aware of things, sometimes it was scary. She loved the way he was casually showing affection at every turn. That had to mean something. Didn't it? Time would tell.

She moved quickly, preparing for the trip, then decided she'd better call her brothers to check on the situation with their father. She'd let them know she was coming to the hospital, but she wouldn't mention the group she was bringing with her. Hopefully she could arrive at a time they weren't there. She didn't want her brothers involved. There was too much bad blood between the families.

It was Marque who answered when she called.

"How's Father?" she asked him.

"I don't really know. We haven't been over to see him in a few days."

"Why not?"

"We've been busy."

Sure. She could just imagine. "Doing what?"

Marque sighed with annoyance. "You know, unlike you, lazing about in the palace doing nothing, we're warriors for the cause. We have things we have to do to prepare for the invasion."

The invasion. Right. You couldn't pick up a tabloid without seeing at least one of her brothers living the high life with the jet set. You didn't see many pictures of them in camouflage or assault gear.

"You and Ivan are too cozy with the playboy lifestyle to be serious warriors and you know it."

"That's not true." His tone said he was mightily insulted by her accusation.

"I'll prove it to you," she said. "When I left there were still negotiations going with neighboring countries to help the Acredonnas. A couple of them would be happy to help you if they could get cut in on the action. Carnethia has the potential to be a rich little country. The resources are here and the people are educated. The infrastructure was damaged by the war, but once that can be repaired, the sky is the limit. All you need to do is show up at a meeting or two. But where are the two of you? Flying off to New York and London, playing the aggrieved rebels in clubs and at dinner parties, instead of taking care of business."

"You have to let negotiations simmer along until they're ripe," he protested. "If you're going to conquer a man like Dane—"

"All you've conquered lately are the front pages of the tabloids. You may not be first in the hearts of the Carnethian people, but the paparazzi are behind you all the way."

"Wow, Alex. You've changed. I don't think you're behind the cause at all anymore."

"Maybe not." She sighed. Maybe not. "I just wanted to let you know I'm going to see Father tomorrow. Don't feel you have to be there. In fact, I'd rather see him on my own."

"No problem," Marque said airily. "Ivan and I have a tennis match at the club, so I don't think we could make it, anyway."

She had to laugh. Disgusted as she was with her brothers and how they were acting, it was probably for the best. They weren't going to pose a real threat to Dane and his rule as long as they refused to grow up.

She went back to packing baby things and preparing for the trip.

They arrived in Paris in late afternoon and checked into a suite in an obscure, backwater hotel where they hoped to remain anonymous. The entourage settled in and Alex prepared to go alone to the hospital.

"I'll go with you," Dane said.

She looked up, alarmed. "But my brothers…"

"I can handle your brothers," he said with a hint of scorn. "I'm not going to let you go alone. I don't have to go into your father's room and upset him. But I want to be there in case you need me."

He dressed simply and pulled a cap down low over his eyes. She laughed when she saw him. They took a cab across town, looking like two normal tourists in Paris.

It was a busy hospital. Nurses and technicians were bustling in and out of rooms, up and down the hallways.

"Can you suggest a quiet place where my friend can wait while I visit my father?" she asked the desk attendant.

"Of course. Right this way."

The room was long and filled with couches and vending machines.

"I guess this will be okay," she said. "I won't be long."

"Good." He pulled her to him and kissed her soundly. "I'll be waiting."

She smiled up at him and just as she began to break away, a form detached itself from the shadows in the far side of the room, and suddenly there was Ivan, a gun in his hand.

"When I heard Alex was coming I had a feeling you might come along for the ride," he said, looking slightly demented. He waved the gun at Dane. "Come to gloat, have you? Come to laugh in our faces now that we're outside and you're on the inside?"

Dane had gone rock hard, and the first thing he did was push Alex behind him.

"Put the gun down," he said. "Let's talk about this."

"Talk!" The gun was pointed right at his chest. "We don't talk, Dane my friend. We fight. Happens every time we meet. We're fated to be enemies for all time, aren't we?"

"No," Dane said. "Listen, Ivan…"

"I'm not listening to you. You stabbed me that day at Kerstin Castle. You cut me and when I fell, you left me there to bleed to death. I saw you saunter out to your fancy army car and drive off. Now I get to take my revenge for that."

"Ivan, don't be a fool!" Alex cried, pushing her way back to the front. "He didn't leave you to bleed to death. If it weren't for him you'd be dead today. He's the one who saved you. When I pulled him out of the wreck of his vehicle, the first thing he did was tell me my brother was up in Kerstin Castle. He was half-dead himself, but he insisted I send help to you, first thing."

Ivan shook his head. "You expect me to believe that? If that was the truth, why didn't you tell me before?"

Alex shook her head. "Because I couldn't admit I had hidden Dane in the barn and was helping him recover from the wounds *you* inflicted on *him*."

Ivan scowled. "You mean he was in that barn the whole time? If I'd known…"

"You'd have killed him," she said flatly.

Ivan shrugged. "Well, sure. There was a war on, you know. Anyway, how do I know you're not just making this up right now to save your boyfriend's life?"

She threw up her hands. "Think what you want, Ivan. I know the truth and so do you, deep down."

"Enough talk," he said, waving the gun at her. "Move out of the way. I don't want to hit you when I kill this guy."

She frowned at him. A part of her didn't believe he would really do this. And yet, how could she know for sure?

"Ivan, meet Dane halfway. He came here with me to see Father. He's ready to offer his hand in reconciliation."

"Am I?" Dane asked softly, looking bemused.

"Reconciliation is for losers," Ivan

sneered. "We may be out of luck right now, but we aren't losers."

"Value judgments are tricky things," Dane murmured.

Alex shot him a scowl. He wasn't helping.

"Ivan, we want to draw people together, not pull them apart."

"Fine words. Sounds good. But emotions can't be doused that easily." He shook his head. "I've been waiting a long, long time for this." He raised the gun, ready to use it. "My turn."

"Hold it," Dane said, and he began to walk toward Alex's brother with steady determination. "Give me the gun."

"Get back!" Ivan shouted. "I'll shoot you both!"

Alex held her breath. She wasn't sure he wouldn't. But just before Dane reached him, the door behind Ivan came swinging open as a nurse came bustling in, hitting him in the back and sending him sprawling.

Dane move quickly, grabbing the gun and putting a foot onto Ivan's back, holding him down.

"I'm sure you have some sort of security

guard nearby," he said to the startled nurse. "It might be an opportune time to call him over."

Alex finally got in to see her father. He was barely conscious. It was evident he didn't have long to live. But he recognized her and squeezed her hand as she whispered loving remembrances in his ear. All in all, she was satisfied.

"Ready to go?" she asked Dane as he met her outside the door to her father's room.

"Yes. I made a statement to the police. They'll hold Ivan for a while, but I doubt he'll get any real jail time. We may have to deal with your brothers again in the future."

She sighed. "I'm afraid you're right."

Her cell phone rang. It was Grace.

"What's happened?" she said as she flipped it open quickly, her heart fluttering. "Is Robbie okay?"

"He's fine," Grace said, her voice lilting. "Do you have a radio with you? Turn it on!"

A radio? Alex looked around the floor but she didn't see a radio.

"Why?"

"They're replaying the crown prince's

broadcast to the people of Carnethia. Alex, you've got to hear this."

"But we don't have a radio!" she wailed. "What did he say?"

"Uh…I think you'd best be ready for a surprise," was all Grace would tell her.

"If you want to know what I said," Dane suggested stolidly, his hands shoved deep into his pockets. "Why not ask me? I happen to be an expert on the subject."

"Oh." Alex rang off from Grace and turned to face him. "Okay, let's have it," she said impatiently.

He smiled at her eagerness. "Okay, here it is. I was open and honest, just as you told me to be. I told them about Robbie and explained how I felt about you."

"Me?" She looked at him, wide-eyed.

"You." He dropped a kiss on the top of her head. "I told them of my intention to ask you to be my wife."

She gasped, hand over her mouth.

"I announced a referendum which will be held this weekend, giving them a few days to think it over, asking their permission to have you as their queen. And I explained that it was their choice, but I was going to marry you, regardless." He smiled at her shocked face. "If you'll have me. And if they don't agree, I'll abide by their wishes. I'll abdicate and Nico will become king."

"In other words?" she said faintly, afraid to take too much for granted.

"In other words, I love you, Alexandra. I want to marry you. I want to have you by my side for the rest of my life. What do you say?"

She could hardly breathe, but she managed one word.

"Yes." She beamed at him, then threw her arms around his neck and hugged for all she was worth. "Oh, yes!"

EPILOGUE

RED and gold banners fluttered everywhere all across the city. A Viennese waltz—the official anthem of the Montenevada family, written for them by Johann Strauss himself in the nineteenth century—could be heard up and down most streets, and everywhere, it seemed, people were dancing.

"I feel like we're living in a dream," Alex murmured as they rode in the elaborate open carriage, drawn by six matching horses and attended by footmen in livery. She could see the golden cathedral ahead, the destination of this coronation parade.

"As long as we get our happy ending, I can live with it," Dane told her with a grin. He wanted to take her in his arms, but his chest was festooned with so much hardware, he clanked when he moved, and her dress was encrusted with diamonds and rubies, making it impossible for her to bend. There had been serious talk of having a crane to hoist her up the cathedral steps in case the dress proved too heavy to walk in. So they had to be content with smiling at each other across the royal barriers.

Music was everywhere, along with shouts of congratulations and good cheer. They rode through the streets of their city, swaying as the horses jogged along, and basked in pure golden happiness.

Alex could hardly believe this was really happening. Just two weeks before, she'd been a captive in an obscure part of the royal palace, hidden from view and locked in frustration. And now she was about to be crowned Queen of Carnethia.

She'd already married her prince earlier that morning in a solemn ceremony at the very same cathedral where they were about to officially take their place in the long line of Carnethian kings and queens. What sort of miracle had allowed her such happiness?

It wasn't a miracle, though. It was Dane.

His broadcast to the people had done the trick. Once they'd heard his words and mulled them over for a day or two, they'd gone to the polls in droves to let him know they were behind him.

"It was your idea," he told her. "You're the one who convinced me that complete honesty with my people would draw them into the decision process and help me make the right choice."

"Yes, but it was your words and your candor that did the trick."

The people of Carnethia loved him as they had never loved the Acredonnas. She knew that. Dane was being magnanimous to her family. She only hoped they appreciated it and didn't do anything to destroy his good will toward them. She knew she would do her part.

But she was a Montenevada now. That made a difference. She told herself that the losers always had more anger and the winners could afford to be magnanimous, but she knew it was more than that. Dane was just a better person.

His words had been reprinted and re-broadcast everywhere, including the

Internet where it was accessible to everyone. The people had voted overwhelmingly to do things his way. His introduction of baby Robbie had struck a chord with Carnethians.

"He may have been born out of wedlock, but he was born as part of a dynasty, and his destiny is to bring together the warring factions of this country. Through him we will find peace, forgiveness, harmony. Through him we will find our way as a great country among the other countries of the world."

Those had been the most important words in his address to the people. She saw the words being quoted everywhere. And now, everywhere she looked, people were holding up teddy bears with Robbie's name on them. They had taken her baby to their hearts, and that brought a shimmer of moisture to her eyes.

"Hey, King Dane," she said, laughing through her tears.

"Hey yourself, Queen Alexandra," he shot back, gazing at her. "Are you ready for this fairy tale to move on to its natural conclusion?"

"You mean the part where we promise

each other a 'happily ever after' life?" she said. "I'm ready."

His smile caught her up in his royal magic. "Good. Because, lady, here it comes."

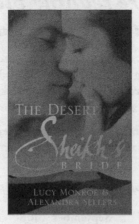

Celebrate 100 years of pure reading pleasure with Mills & Boon®

To mark our centenary, each month we're publishing a special 100th Birthday Edition. These celebratory editions are packed with extra features and include a FREE bonus story.

Plus, you have the chance to enter a fabulous monthly prize draw. See 100th Birthday Edition books for details.

Now that's worth celebrating!

September 2008

Crazy about her Spanish Boss by Rebecca Winters
Includes FREE bonus story
Rafael's Convenient Proposal

November 2008

**The Rancher's Christmas Baby
by Cathy Gillen Thacker**
Includes FREE bonus story *Baby's First Christmas*

December 2008

One Magical Christmas by Carol Marinelli
Includes FREE bonus story *Emergency at Bayside*

Look for Mills & Boon® 100th Birthday Editions at your favourite bookseller or visit
www.millsandboon.co.uk

4 FREE

BOOKS AND A SURPRISE GIFT!

We would like to take this opportunity to thank you for reading this Mills & Boon® book by offering you the chance to take FOUR more specially selected titles from the Romance series absolutely FREE! We're also making this offer to introduce you to the benefits of the Mills & Boon® Book Club—

- ★ FREE home delivery
- ★ FREE gifts and competitions
- ★ FREE monthly Newsletter
- ★ Exclusive Mills & Boon® Book Club offers
- ★ Books available before they're in the shops

Accepting these FREE books and gift places you under no obligation to buy, you may cancel at any time, even after receiving your free shipment. Simply complete your details below and return the entire page to the address below. You don't even need a stamp!

YES! Please send me 4 free Romance books and a surprise gift. I understand that unless you hear from me, I will receive 6 superb new titles every month for just £2.99 each, postage and packing free. I am under no obligation to purchase any books and may cancel my subscription at any time. The free books and gift will be mine to keep in any case.

N8ZED

Ms/Mrs/Miss/Mr ....Initials ....
BLOCK CAPITALS PLEASE

Surname ....

Address ....

....

....Postcode..

Send this whole page to:
UK: FREEPOST CN81, Croydon, CR9 3WZ